MANY WORLDS

MANY WORLDS:

SOME

AMERICAN

ODYSSEYS

short stories & illustrations by

M. Kaat Toy

Shanti Arts Publishing
Brunswick, Maine

MANY WORLDS: SOME AMERICAN ODYSSEYS

Published by Shanti Arts Publishing
Illustrations, including cover, by M. Kaat Toy
Design by Shanti Arts Designs

Shanti Arts LLC
Brunswick, Maine
www.shantiarts.com

Printed in the United States of America

ISBN: 978-1-951651-57-2 (softcover)
ISBN: 978-1-951651-58-9 (ebook)

Library of Congress Control Number: 2020950800

There are many worlds, but they are in this one.

Contents

Acknowledgments

Grateful acknowledgment is made to the editors of the following publications where these stories first appeared:

Another Chicago Magazine: "Feng Shui" (1999)

Black Warrior Review: "Subvert-Yr-Cat" (1990)

Boston Review: "The Need for Light" (1990)

Cimarron Review: "Saving Herself for Julian Markov" (2004)

Coe Review: "In The People's Art Museum" (2012)

Concho River Review: "Family Business" (2013)

The Dos Passos Review: "Knowledge of Material Limitations" (2013–14)

Elixir: "Intuition or Imagination?" (2008)

Fiction: "Any Failure to Obey Orders Will Be Considered an Act of Aggression" (1998) and "Red Boots" (2000)

Kansas Quarterly: "The Dangers of Disease" published as "Pictures of Family Life" (1990)

Kingfisher: "Mr. Mystery's Victory" published as "Notes from an Interview" (1987)

Mademoiselle: "Hot Ticket to Nowhere" published as "In the Land of the Married" (1988)

The Missouri Review: "The Boys from This School" (1987)

The Mochila Review: "Boundary Lines" (2010)

Pacific Review: "Of Chemistry and Geography" (2004-05)

Pilgrimage: "Say It Ain't So" (2010)

Provincetown Arts: "Justice" (2000)

The Southern Anthology: "Big Mama's" (1994), nominated for the Pushcart Prize

Still Point Arts Quarterly: "The Circles They Swam In" (2020)

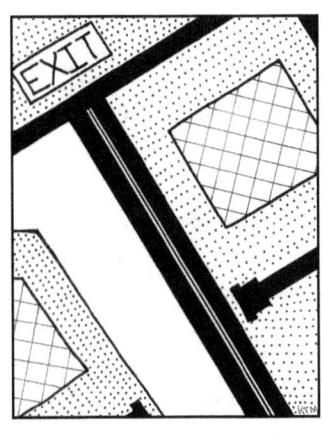

Mr. Mystery's Victory

"THE WORDS CREATE THE IMAGE of the words," my writing professor says. The words I choose to tell this story make it appear humorous, pathetic. The events are humorous, pathetic. They are also random, yet order can be imposed on them. Ordering is the process of leaving out that which does not contribute to order, although what is left out may be interesting, may contribute to an understanding of the whole.

I've been looking at the events, the pictures they appear as, for two weeks now. I've tried to impose logic, system, especially a positive system of logic on them and to make them recur—physically not just mentally—or at least continue to occur as they would in a story so I can write a story about them. The events refuse to continue. This is because they involve a person, and persons tend to resist being the objects of other people's stories, though they like to tell stories and are constantly placing themselves in them.

There is a guy, my age—an apparently young age but really a few years older—leaning forward on his toes and opening with one arm the green metal door in the tan hallway of a major southwestern university. For some, the fact this occurs in a major university lends importance to the guy, the door, the hallway, the story; but those who think major universities important generally demand the stories they will listen to be more than pictures. People at universities like action; they are generally there for the action; they find action, of various sorts, there.

The guy is short, blond with an intellectually high forehead. He is a participant, occasionally, in the myth of the importance of this university, but that's not what is interesting about him. What is interesting is the beautifully sculpted muscles in his arms, his thinning blond hair, the little unattractive tuft of hair underneath his lip and why it is there. Presumably he could shave it. Presumably he likes it. He is a poet, this short blond fellow, presumably one in pursuit of beauty, and yet he likes this ugly tuft of hair as a discordant element upon his face.

What is also interesting is that while tuition and student loan costs increased and education grants were defunded, he went to Maine—presumably in search of poems, adventure, the 1960s. Perhaps it is my fantasy about him that is interesting. Perhaps he is not interesting at all, but it is an important part of my fantasy that life can be interesting—as seems to be evidenced by some people—and not merely strange.

This interview contains one embarrassing question. Not that only one question was embarrassing, but there was only one question, and it was embarrassing. That is another problem with this interview, with every encounter I have had recently that has potential for an interview. We are all in a hurry, we have important things to do—we whose purpose is to function for this university.

"Did you make any money while you were in Maine?" I asked.

I didn't care if he made any money. He didn't care if he made any money. That is part of what holds us together here at the university: Everyone has agreed not to care if anyone makes any money. Outside, there is money to be made, thought about, spent, worried about. Inside, there is not. I wanted to explain that I understood this, I accepted this, after I asked my one question, but there was no time to explain.

I suppose you are wondering what has happened to the door. Has it opened or shut? Has the young man come in or gone out? Can a short fellow, even a short fellow with beautifully muscled arms, hold a door this long? I forget. There is more conversation, but I'm not sure how it relates to the opening of the door—before or after. Anyway, this is what he did in Maine: For one month he hauled boxes of open cans of sardines lying greased together in their graves from one cannery table to another. Those fish stunk, he told me; then, he said he learned some things but was not specific.

One more thing seems interesting. As far as I can tell, this person never feels guilty: not about the sardines, or the toilets he cleaned to support himself his first year in graduate school, or the fact that he was still looking for somewhere to live that first week after school started, walking down the hallway asking if anyone knew of a place—cheap. Imagine what your mother would say, my mother would say, probably what his mother would say if she were alive, if she knew that her son—at that age, and with that much education, and such a bright boy, and not bad looking if he'd only dress right, wear something besides sweatshirts for Christ's sake, he's teaching at a major university—one week into the semester of his third year of graduate school didn't have a place to live. And didn't feel guilty.

So I had all this saved up to talk about later, maybe in his office, in my office, in between classes, and this is the next picture, even briefer, with less action than the last one. About a week later he is standing at his mailbox in the English office where faculty—yes, faculty—get their mail, which is what he is doing. Though he is not facing my way, I know it is him because of the sweatshirt, the thinning hair, the wonderfully muscular arms.

"Oh boy!" I say. "It's Mr. Mystery, and we're going to play!" I put a finger into each of his sides.

"Oh no, we're not," Mr. Mystery says. "Mr. Mystery doesn't want to play."

And Mr. Mystery goes back to skimming his mail, turns, and walks out of this interview forever. Mr. Mystery goes into one of the inner offices, one of the special places for special people, inside the English department of this important institution, and presumably goes on to hear other words, better questions, words presumably more to his liking, spoken by more important people who deal with things more effectively, while I stand lost in mine.

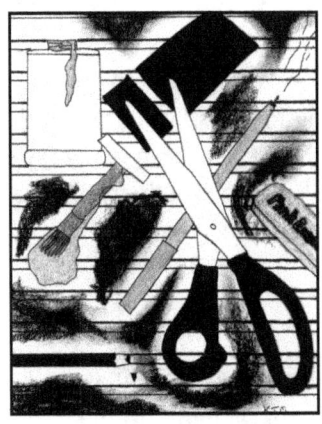

Justice

MONDAY, SARAH, THE PRINT supervisor in a Los Angeles print production center, notices the new young graphic designer, Jill, talking to a delivery boy just out of high school waiting for summer to end so he can play college football. Mike, with his beefy arms folded across his beefy chest, seems to have the muscles and the confidence. Jill, with her round breasts thrust up and her round butt thrust out, smiles at him like a doll-shaped sucker waiting to be licked, an obsequious pose she never concocts for Sarah.

"Jill, you'd better get those ads done," Sarah shouts as she throws down a stack of shiny circulars on the counter.

Jill smiles and motions her hand in Sarah's direction but keeps talking. Sarah looks at her again. Jill waves goodbye to Mike and sits at her computer. Soon Sarah sees Jill laughing with the secretary. Sarah wraps a string around the circulars and pulls until the string breaks.

"Ey, *mi novia*," Carlos, a little Chicano guy, says to Sarah as he stacks circulars on a dolly. "*Una mal chica.*" He nods toward Jill.

Sarah smiles at him and reties the string.

In the courtyard of Sarah's apartment complex, her neighbor boys, Lonnie and Nicholas, play. The brothers are blue-eyed towheads but look nothing alike.

Nicholas, the younger one with a round baby face, the one she likes best, asks, "Can I wash your car?"

Lonnie, whose face is thin and oval, adopts a girlish pout as he pulls the petals off a flower he picked from the flower bed. Lonnie doesn't like to wash cars.

Sarah shakes her head. "No, it's too late." It's almost dark.

"*Uuhhhh,*" Nicholas says, slapping his forehead. "We're bored."

Their mother, a former drug addict, raised them in welfare motels. Now a Christian fundamentalist, she still doesn't have enough money to keep them entertained. They don't even have bicycles.

"I'm sorry," Sarah says.

That evening she watches something on TV taking place at a home for battered children, perhaps a light drama. The children play touch football on the lawn with their crutches and broken arms while their parents, supervised by a counselor, have breakdowns and confrontations on the office couch. The doorbell rings. Sarah gets up to answer it.

"Can we play with your computer?" Lonnie asks.

"No. It isn't working." The mouse needs batteries.

"Well, can we color then?" Nicholas says.

She lets them in. They run across the room to her art supplies.

"Does your mother know you're here?"

Nicholas makes big eyes at Sarah and nods. "She told us to come here."

This is probably a lie, but if Sarah calls his mother and it is, he'll get in trouble.

A few minutes later she tapes Nicholas's picture of an American flag with pink stars and green stripes to her refrigerator.

Lonnie comes in with a drawing of her with a nose like a pig and a smile like a watermelon-shaped slice of board fence: "Sarah is pretty," it says.

"That's nice," she tells Lonnie.

"*Zack* is the *best* artist in my class," he says. "*And* he is the cutest boy. I just *love* him." He rolls his eyes and gazes at the ceiling.

In the morning Sarah finds Jill talking to Mike again. Bundles of circulars wait to be taken to the loading dock. Sarah watches

Mike and Jill kiss goodbye. She has also watched Jill kiss her boyfriend goodbye. It looks the same.

That afternoon when Sarah opens the composing room door, Jill and Mike are making out in the corner. They smile at her. She closes the door and waits for them to come out.

The chief of operations, Mr. Reynolds, walks by. "What's going on, Sarah?"

"Oh, nothing. Just waiting for something to develop."

"Well, find something to do."

"Sure, okay."

After he leaves, Sarah opens the door again.

"Get the hell out of there," she yells.

Jill giggles as Mike's belt buckle drops against the concrete. Sarah shuts the door.

When they come out, Sarah says, "All right, you guys. I don't want this to happen again."

"Sure, okay," Mike says. He puts his arm around Jill and cocks his head up at Sarah.

Mr. Reynolds comes over again. "Jill, I've been looking for you. Could you come to my office for a minute? I've got a new ad campaign I want to discuss with you."

"Certainly, Mr. Reynolds." Jill smiles at Sarah then at Mike. Mike takes his hand off her butt.

"I'd just love to work on a new project," Sarah hears Jill say to Mr. Reynolds as they walk away.

Lonnie and Nicholas are wandering around the carport when Sarah drives in.

"Take us to McDonald's!" Nicholas yells, running toward her car.

"I don't have any money." She had to have her car repaired, and that emptied her checking account. She cut up her credit card so she wouldn't overspend.

"Yes, you do," Lonnie says in a snooty tone, one hand on his hip, one shoulder thrust forward, his nose in the air. "You just don't like us."

"She likes us," Nicholas says. "She's the only friend we've got."

She invites them in for ice tea. They watch as she assembles everything.

"This is pretty," Lonnie says, tracing over the design on the china sugar bowl. He holds it over the floor. "If I drop it, it would break, huh?"

She wants to grab it from him. He pours sugar onto the linoleum.

"Lonnie, clean that up!" she shouts.

Lonnie shakes his head, puts the bowl on the counter, and runs out the door.

"I'll clean it up," Nicholas says. "I always have to clean up after him. He's lazy." He heads to the broom closet, walking like a farmer going to pitch hay. He never misses an opportunity to be cute.

The next day Jill calls in sick. Sarah goes to Jill's computer to compose some posters Jill was supposed to do. On the company's website, Jill has set up her own page, complete with her color photograph and vital statistics.

After Sarah finishes Jill's work, she skips lunch to do some offset printing. Carrying a large digitally imaged aluminum plate into the composing room, she trips on a box of chemicals, dropping the plate, her chin hitting the concrete. She certainly didn't put that box in the middle of the floor.

She goes to talk to Mr. Reynolds.

"I've had a lot of bad reports about Jill," he says, "but I think people are just jealous. She's a very attractive girl, you know. It sounds like a personal problem to me."

Sarah nods, her hands and chin throbbing from her fall.

When she gets home she looks in the bathroom mirror. Her chin has blossomed into a plum.

At breakfast there are no eggs and no milk, so she has corn flakes with orange juice on them. Tomorrow will be pay day. Still hungry, she mixes up sugar, cornstarch, and water, cooks it, and eats that. When did she ever have money to buy cornstarch?

As she washes her damaged face, she remembers she's

going to have to talk to Jill. She wants to tell her she's a stupid slut, but that doesn't sound too professional. How else can she put it? She would tell Jill she will get rid of her if she doesn't straighten up, but can she get rid of her? Mr. Reynolds likes Jill.

When she gets to work, Sarah opens the back door to the loading dock. Jill and Mike stand near the dumpster making out.

"Jill, could I talk to you?" Sarah asks.

Jill looks at Mike then at Sarah. "Could it wait?"

"No, I don't think so."

"Okay. See you in a few, Mike."

"Morning, boss," Mike says as he slips inside.

"I haven't done anything wrong, have I?" Jill inquires. "Mr. Reynolds thinks I'm doing a really good job."

"Yeah, well, there's just a few things. Like the other night you left a box out in the composition room."

"Oh, I didn't leave it out. Mike did. My boyfriend was waiting, and it was time to punch out. I told Mike to put it back. It wasn't my fault."

"Maybe you and Mike shouldn't be in there together."

"But Mr. Reynolds said I should get familiar with all the facilities. Mike was showing me where things are. You don't have a problem with that, do you?"

Sarah shakes her head. Finally, she says, "You know, your job doesn't really require that you have a webpage on our website."

"But Mr. Reynolds told me that he wants me to know about all the technology. He sees a big future for me here. You could ask him. I know he'd agree. Was there anything else?"

"No. Just be careful around the composition room. And try to do something productive during the time you're being paid."

"Well, I will and thank you for talking to me. I certainly want us to get along because I have to work for you."

"Yeah," Sarah says, though it hardly seems true.

"I'd better go. Mike'll be waiting."

At lunch Sarah sees Jill and Mr. Reynolds walking out of his office toward the front door.

After work Sarah drives around wondering what to do. She doesn't want to see tonight's sitcom, *Fiesta U*. It makes her sick watching all those fraternity and sorority kids making out during lectures and drag racing through stoplights in their convertibles. She sees a laundromat and stops. Someone told her about finding three dollars in change at one.

Inside, she gets on her knees and begins moving down the rows, sticking her hands under the machines and in the spaces between them. People come and go, but all she sees are their shoes. She's impressed by a nasty pair of black patent leather pumps with pointed toes and a strap back, but when she looks up, the girl wearing them could only be twelve or thirteen.

A short scrawny man comes in wearing dirty pants and carrying a laundry bag over his shoulder. He walks up to the laundry aids machine and pulls the knobs.

"Fuck this shit," he says. "I don't need this information."

She smiles at him. Her knees are sore and she's covered with lint. She found two quarters and a dime. She gets up, brushes herself off, and sneezes.

Fuck this shit. I don't need this information, she tells herself as she follows him to the exit.

Friday, Mr. Reynolds announces there will be no paychecks. A computer broke down in the corporate office. Sarah has no food for the weekend. During the morning she finds Jill and Mike making out in the composition room, the paper storage area, and behind the stacks of paper to be recycled.

She goes through her desk and finds some change, so for lunch she walks to the quick store. She gets a Coke and a package of Zingers, the most calories for the dollar. One aisle over she sees two heads, one dark-haired and one straw-white, leaning together. She thinks it is Mike and Jill and wants to throw her Zingers at them. She walks around and sees it is two teen-aged boys looking at comic books.

Back in the lunch room everyone is talking about where they've seen Mike and Jill making out.

"I saw them go into the women's room."

"I saw them in the men's room."

"I saw them getting into the delivery van one afternoon. It must have been a hundred degrees out there."

"The delivery guys laugh whenever they see Mike," an old guy says. "They follow him around and say, 'Where's Jill? *A boomba, boomba*' and hold their hands out like big breasts and wiggle."

Even Sarah laughs.

Jill and Mr. Reynolds come to the door. Jill smiles at everyone. Mr. Reynolds says, "Glad to see you're having a good time. Maybe you'll do more work this afternoon." He leaves.

Jill sits down. "He is so stud," she says, observing the ceiling. She could be talking about Mr. Reynolds or Mike or someone she just met. No one knows how to answer her, and soon everyone drifts off.

Sarah is called to the counter when one of their regular customers, Bill, a lawyer, comes to check his ad advertising his legal rates. Bill has on yellow slacks, a green-and-black plaid shirt, and a brown sport coat. Sarah cannot figure out his coordinating principle.

He asks if she wants to go to dinner. He has asked before. This time she says yes. It is the only way she can think of to get a meal. Other women go out with guys for their money all the time, she tells herself.

After he leaves, she heads for the composing room. The door is shut, so she knocks and shouts, "Hey, get dressed. I'm coming in."

When she opens the door, Mike and Jill aren't there. She goes in but turns around when she hears them walking by. They lift their hands to show they aren't touching and laugh at her. Aligning the developed pages in the stripper, her hands shake so much she has to give up.

In the main room she loads circulars onto a dolly next to Carlos.

"*Como está?*" Carlos says.

"*Estoy* sick and tired of this shit."

"El trabajo?"

"No, la bruja, la mujera rubia."

"Do you want to come for dinner *en mi casa*?" Carlos says.

"I have a date."

"Ah, *bien*. You're not looking so good these days anyway."

"Thanks a big fucking lot."

"Ah, *mi novia, mi amor*." Carlos clutches his heart.

On her way home Sarah sees a small blonde on a bicycle ahead of her. She thinks it's Jill. She looks around her car for something to throw at her. She wishes she had a cup of Coke, but all she has is a rock. She turns to follow the bicycle. When she goes by, the young woman smiles. It isn't Jill. It takes Sarah ten minutes to get back to her street.

An hour before Bill is supposed to arrive, Sarah lets the boys color in her living room while she goes into the bathroom, pours peroxide in a cup, and dips the ends of her straight brown hair into it. She watches in the mirror as the bottom half of her hair turns yellow-orange. Lonnie comes in. He looks at the barrettes and hair clips in her drawer longingly. He picks up an elaborate gold one and strokes it. He sees her watching him.

"I can't have this," he tells her as if someone has already told him, "because I'm a boy, and boys don't wear these." He throws it in the drawer, slams the drawer shut, and runs back to the living room.

After the boys leave, Sarah is in her bedroom getting dressed when she hears a noise in the living room. She walks in buttoning her shirt, her jeans unzipped.

"Hi," Bill says as if they are best friends.

They go to a pizza place Bill likes because it's cheap. He spent the morning serving eviction papers he tells her, his favorite part of his job. He talks about the money he gets for different legal chores and how much he saves at a warehouse supermarket buying in bulk.

When the waitress drops off the tab, Sarah insists on paying so she won't owe Bill a thing. She writes a bad check. Her bank will cover it, but it'll cost. Bill is so grateful she thinks she'll have to slap his face.

On the drive back to her apartment, he asks if he can come in for coffee.

"We don't even like each other," she says.

He reluctantly agrees but still wants to come up.

"I hate you," she tells him.

"That bad?" he asks.

She nods.

To make sure she doesn't get forced into anything, as he slows to a stop at her building she opens the door and jumps out. She runs inside, locks the door, and turns on the lights.

The boys are soon knocking. She sits outside on the steps with them enjoying the cool night air.

"When you're in your emotional wheelchair, you can go to the emotional wheelchair campground, and they'll take care of you for the weekend," Nicholas tells her.

"That's stupid," Lonnie says.

"Or else if you're blind, they'll let you bring a seeing eye hamster to the park as long as you keep him on a leash. You can go on nature walks. There's piles of corn at all the stops, and you can touch the trees and plants and things."

Nicholas wants to get his baseball and play catch, so they walk toward the boys' apartment. Lonnie hangs back. He doesn't want to play catch. Sarah waits for him while Nicholas runs ahead.

"Watch me," Lonnie says. He walks on his tiptoes as if he's wearing high heels. His hips sway, and he waves his hands, limp-wristed, in flourishes to each side.

"I *have* to walk like this," he tells her.

She knows, in a way, it's true. He crosses the whole courtyard without letting his heels touch the ground.

Nicholas comes out with his baseball. Lonnie straightens up.

"When I get paid, I'll take you guys to McDonald's," she says, catching Nicholas's toss. She can't afford it, but she doesn't care.

"Yeah!" Nicholas shouts.

"But *I* don't like McDonald's," Lonnie whines. "Can't we go somewhere *I* want to go?"

"Shut up, Lonnie. You do too like McDonald's," Nicholas says.

Sarah smiles at them. She is giving up on justice. Things are never going to turn out fair.

Family Business

IN THE KITCHEN OF THE ORDINARY embattled house where I grew up, at least one morning a week for years, twenty pounds or more of pinto beans simmered alongside the fried eggs and bacon—beans in a pot so big it spread over two of the gas burners, hung over the edge of the stove, bumped into my mother's frying pan, into her fingers and burned them—beans for at least two hundred people my father would serve at a barbecue that night in our central California town.

The beans smelled like boiled dish rags or garbage, and by the time I got to breakfast I'd be nauseous and angry. At 7:30 my father, large and in a hurry, finished his eggs, mopped his plate with his toast, straightened his dark tie against a white shirt my mother had ironed Sunday night, sipped his coffee, then kissed me on the cheek, his lips wet and his breath darkly smoky. He went over to the beans, stirred down the brown foam, laid the dripping spoon on the stove, patted my temperamental mother on the rear, kissed her, then headed to the door, on his way to earning his fortune.

She was his helpmate, helping him. "Jake, what do I do with these beans!" she called out to him.

He stopped and turned around at the door to speak, or if he had gotten as far as the yard, he shouted, "If I'm not back, turn them off around noon."

I thought she called to him to repeat the instructions

because she couldn't remember, but of course it was more complicated than that.

"God damn beans!" she screamed when he was gone. She smashed the long wooden spoon against the rim of the pan, stomped the floor, then maybe cried at the sink.

I stopped eating and wanted to throw the beans out, heave the giant pot onto the patio, get rid of the arguments and the smell, but there were other people to think of, my parents had instilled in me, the people who would be eating the beans.

As I finished breakfast, my brother, Jimmy, older by eight years, would walk in, lanky and aloof, rubbing his eyes, late for high school.

"Beans again?" he would say then argue with our mother about his breakfast or his life.

Now I am in the kitchen of my parents' new house. Because I live three thousand miles away, I haven't been here before. My mother tidies up as I heat water for the beans we will serve my parents' guests tonight. I hold ice from the automatic ice maker on my finger that I burned on the electric stove. I can't find the potholders or get the water to boil.

"That burner has a short in it," she says.

"It works. I just burned my finger on it."

"It works. It just doesn't get hot enough for water to boil." She peers into the pot then at me through steamed-up glasses and smiles.

I wrap a potholder around the ice on my finger, move the pan to another burner, and wait for the beans to simmer.

My father walks in and watches as I salt them then looks in the pot and salts them again. I hope he is not trying to sabotage me.

"Are you sure they needed that?" I ask.

"Of course. Who's the head cook around here anyway?" He looks down at my mother and me then stirs the pot once. "Good luck, girls." He goes back to the TV.

The beans start to foam, but because there is a powerful

fan over the stove, the kitchen does not smell like fermenting trash. It smells like nothing at all.

In high school my father worked at the small grocery store my mother's fierce German father owned and my mother had no fondness for. After high school, my father joined the Army. In Texas he learned to barbecue. Returning, he married my mother and took over the store. In the butcher shop were the butcher's block and all the butcher's tools—sharp fast tools for turning out work. I watched as he sliced bologna into piles on the sliding circular saw or ground hamburger, stuffing scraps of meat into the machine with a wooden mallet, forcing it out in long noodley red threads. The back room had a gray sheet metal sink I was afraid to get near because of its rotten metallic smell, a meat locker where my father stored gallons of mayonnaise and cold soup next to whole pigs and lambs, and a tiny gas stove, which was why he sometimes had to take his cooking home.

Besides the beans he made deep-pit barbecue sandwiches for football games, prepared whole beef tongues the local Basque style, and stuffed holiday turkeys for those who could not do it as well. He baked them, too, in his tiny oven for old ladies with their tiny ovens and large families coming to visit. He whistled while carrying sides of beef on his shoulder. If he dropped pimento cheese or potato salad, he rubbed them into the sawdust. When he sliced his finger open, he sucked the blood. My mother could only look disgusted. She couldn't yell at him here.

All day women came in with their special requests: Cornish hens, butterflied roasts, prime rib. My father greeted them from the meat counter, shouting out whatever he had a special on. His favorites were the wives of professional men, attractive and well-groomed, always friendly and laughing at his jokes. He ran their Swiss steak through the tenderizer an extra time or pounded their veal extra thin.

My mother worked the cash register, running interference between my father and the housewives.

"You're so lucky," the women said as she bagged their food, "to have a man who can cook."

My mother smiled and said, "He's a real help," then carried their groceries to their cars.

When Mrs. Bryant came in, a blonde cheerleader-type, the football coach's wife, my father came out from behind the butcher's counter wiping his hands on his meat-stained apron. When she finished shopping, my father carried her groceries out, stacking the bags in his arms.

If he stayed too long in the parking lot, my mother shouted out the door, "Jake, get in here. I can't run this place by myself."

He hopped up the steps, smiling, looking for customers. Sometimes there weren't any. When the Bryants left town, my father was friendly with another blonde, Mrs. O'Neil. My mother was brunette.

When it was quiet, she worked in the back room at the desk where her father once did, keeping track of the money. Though her father used to shout at her and make her cry, his desk was sacred, as was everything on it. I hung between the edges of my grandfather's desk and my father's butcher block.

At the end of the day, my mother went home to fix dinner. I stayed to help my father check out, counting the change and putting it into paper coin rollers to take to the bank. When we went on delivery rounds in his faded yellow truck, the leather seat and dash cracked and blackened, he was still whistling after eleven hours of work.

Our favorite place was Mom's boarding house. There were pots cooking on the stove and covered dishes on the long counter. It made my father happy to see so much of his food prepared for the working men who lived in the house, food like we had—southern, German, or Irish—chicken and biscuits, pot roast, cabbage and corned beef.

At home, my mother scraped our leftovers onto my father's plate. "Finish them up," she said then criticized him for getting fat.

After dinner I sat on my father's lap while we watched TV. He whistled the theme songs and drummed his fingers on my back to the beat.

One or two nights a week, my father stood on the patio of the Elks' Club slapping racks of steaks on the grill. Cooking steaks was what he did best. There were fifty steaks on each rack. There were four racks to turn on a grill twelve feet long. Arching back, he raised each rack. Juice ran down his huge hairy arms or into the flames. The fire flared. As the rack smashed down, sparks and bits of meat and juice flew up. Sparks and sweet gray smoke drifted into the night. He wiped the charcoal and blood from his knife onto his white starched apron, smiled, and cut off a bite. My mother poured ice water or arranged butter pats and stayed clean and far away.

When he shouted that the steaks were ready, the people lined up. My brother arrived just in time to put peas on the plate, for color, or cooked carrots or lima beans. My mother burned her hands serving the baked potatoes.

"These potholders look like hell," she said to my father when she got a chance, "or I'd use one."

People smiled at him when he gave them their steaks, striped red and black from the grill, steaming, thick, and beautiful.

"Good work, Jake," they said. "You're the best."

Later he told us, "I hate it when they compliment me. They think they're doing me some favor, 'Big Jake,' 'Good 'ol Jake,' but they're not."

I served the beans next to the steaks.

Those were the best times I remember my family having. After everyone was served, my father piled up our plates for us and dipped our bread in the steak juice. He paid Jimmy and me a dollar or two, and Jimmy could leave, no questions asked, because we'd all been working. No one felt like a failure, except my mother perhaps, watching her friends eat in the dining room, but I always thought we were special because we'd done the work. It was like we were a real family, like in *Father Knows Best* or *Lassie*.

The summer before his senior year in high school, Jimmy worked at the store full-time. He learned to run the meat grinder and the circular saw. In the fall, hunters brought in deer. Jimmy got mad dressing them because the fleas and chiggers bit him.

He bought a motorcycle with the money he was supposed

to save for college. It was red. My father told him to get rid of the goddamned thing. Jimmy threatened to move out of the house.

"Over my dead body," my mother said.

One night when leaving the store in his truck, my father backed over the motorcycle and crushed it. He never saw it, he said.

Then there was a phone call in the middle of the night. The store was on fire. We got dressed and drove in the truck, the only time I remember all four of us in it. My mother, Jimmy, and I sat in the parking lot watching my father, bare-headed and bare-armed, going in and out of the smoke-filled building well-equipped firemen wouldn't enter, trying to save God knows what, as the flames roared out the windows and burst through the roof.

I screamed and clutched the dashboard, shouting "Why doesn't someone stop him!" My mother glared at me.

Jimmy eased out of the truck and started toward the building, but my mother went after him, making him promise not to go in. Jimmy stood by himself, one hand on his slim hip, while the firemen rushed around, and my mother and I held hands in the truck. My father quit just before the roof crashed in. He stood there watching the store while we watched him, and it grew light.

That morning men helped my father drag out the burnt remains: files of records and receipts, grocery carts with the rubber wheels burned off, the ice cream freezer chest that had short-circuited and started the fire, and my bicycle, a black shell. My father was supposed to bring it home and forgot.

"I'm sorry, honey," he said when he saw me standing beside it. "It's going to be a while before we can afford another one."

I nodded. I knew the business came first.

By afternoon the pile included my grandfather's desk. I cried when I touched its bubbled surface, and my mother put her arm around me.

My father used the insurance money to buy into a profitable beef-processing business. Just like that, I was no longer second heir apparent to the Ideal Market. My father couldn't cut deals for the ladies any more. He tried to do barbecues from our house, but it was too hard. Jimmy went to college in Los Angeles. Now he works on computers. He likes them because they're clean and don't bleed. My mother started going out with the fancy ladies in our town.

I rarely talk about the store; there is little context for it. In college I was a vegetarian for a few months. It took my father years to forgive me. My friends get upset if I remind them their dinner once cackled or chewed its cud. Occasionally I'll tell about gigging frogs for frog legs from the truck, their severed bodies hopping off the tailgate, or having scrambled cow brains with eggs for breakfast and barbecued steer balls for hors d'oeuvres. "Mountain oysters" my mother called them when we had company.

My father keeps in shape walking and doing chores for my mother. His bursitis is gone, and he doesn't have to wear arch supports any more. He barbecues on the gas grill Jimmy bought him. When he carves a roast for visitors, he still points out what cuts were on either side. On the phone last Christmas he told me he wanted to give groceries to some poor family, but he didn't know who to give them to. In their new neighborhood no one is short of food.

On my desk is a wooden recipe box that made it through the fire. It used to hold the store's bad debts—bills customers ran up and couldn't pay. It shows my grandfather's accounting with a grease pencil on the lid. It holds my flash drives. I don't know any kids who help their parents. Most kids don't know what their parents do. Everything is all separate now.

By evening, the beans are ready. My father sprinkles the steaks with seasoned salt until my mother says, "Jake, stop." He dabs at the spill with his finger and licks it. He opens three cans of salsa—two regular, one spicy hot.

"My secret mixture," he tells me. He used to make his own.

"Do you ever miss the store?" I finally have the courage to ask.

"Honey," he says, "it was time for me to get out. I was getting too old to work that hard. We made a lot more money in the new business."

I thought losing the store made my father old. I didn't realize he was getting old anyway.

At dinner, Lenore, the doctor's ex-wife, a tall dramatically beautiful redhead, a favorite of my father's from the old days, asks him if he made the beans.

Before he can answer, I describe when we cooked for and served a thousand people. There were lines everywhere, everyone waiting for my father's food. I thought I might embarrass him, but instead he smiles. His eyebrows lift up. His face gets young and energetic again.

"Do you remember those days?" my mother asks me.

I nod, not wanting to say how much I remember.

Without thinking she says, "I never knew how miserable I was until I got out."

All the conversation stops. My mother looks around defensively. For once she has spoken the truth.

My father looks to me for help. As I start to speak, he watches to make sure I don't cause all those years of her anger to crack.

I close my mouth. Everyone waits. I nod at my mother again, the only one—except my father perhaps—understanding how hard it had been for a woman like her to wait on everyone else.

The Circles They Swam In

FOR LABOR DAY WEEKEND, thirty-five-year-old Gabby—a central LA librarian/caseworker for the dystopically entangled underserved—is getting together with her childhood friends Lindsay and Lindsay's older brother, Peter, in Santa Barbara, a central coast Mediterranean-style city with picturesque red tile roofs required on all public buildings and a policy of no growth. Its motto could be taken from a bumper sticker Gabby saw on a black Jaguar there: "We don't care. We don't have to."

From southern California they are rendezvousing at Gabby's parents' vacation apartment. Peter and Lindsay tried to get hotel rooms for the long weekend, Lindsay explained when she called, but their usual accommodations were taken, so she thought it would be fun for the three of them to get together. This sounded more mannered and predictable than spray painting clothes at her barrio yard sale as Gabby had planned. Reluctantly, she told Lindsay the key's hiding place.

When Gabby arrives at her parents' apartment late Friday afternoon, she finds a shiny silver sports car in the garage. The plate reads "Lin Zs." She thinks it is a Datsun Z then sees it is a Porsche. Gabby's older brother, Geoffrey, was driving a small silver Porsche when he was killed in a car wreck at eighteen. Gabby, ten, was in the apartment with her parents when the highway patrolman arrived and told them he was dead. She went outside, stood on the balcony, and screamed, imagining driving a knife into her heart to stop it from beating, to cut off the feeling part of herself so the rest of her could live. Even now she can see blood on the concrete. It was that real.

Upstairs in the living room with a view of the sea, she finds Lindsay sitting on the couch reading *Santa Barbara Magazine*. On the cover a model who looks like Lindsay wears a brown leather bikini and cowboy hat.

Gabby remembers Lindsay in their eighth-grade graduation picture as an unremarkable adolescent with a bouffant pageboy tied with a pink satin bow. Now Lindsay is tall, slender, and with the help of artificial implants, perfectly built. Her husband, a surgeon fifteen years older than she, is home on call. Lindsay married him for his money, she freely admits. They are building a custom home in the San Gabriel foothills so Lindsay can keep her Thoroughbreds next to the house. Along with money, she has acquired a winning smile—full-lipped but reserved—and a sparkle of success in her narrow green eyes Gabby doesn't remember being there when Lindsay was a child.

Lindsay hops up and gives Gabby a hard nervous hug, actually trembling so her large diamond pendant earrings and even larger diamond ring shake in the slanting summer light. When they graduated high school, Gabby was considered the smart one, destined for success. Seeing Lindsay adorned with diamonds shocks her into realizing she has officially lost the race. She once had such a head start. Now she can't even compete.

The newly redecorated apartment features pearlized beach shell accent colors: shades of pale gold, mauve, and blue. It is immaculate with all the warmth of a luxury hotel suite, which is what it was. Gabby looks toward the kitchen at an array of chips, cookies, and foil-wrapped candies from a gourmet food store on the kitchen counter.

"Do you want something to eat?" Lindsay asks. "I bought some stuff." Lindsay has a speedy metabolism and can eat all day, anything she wants.

Gabby, who has struggled to not be fat since she was three, shakes her head.

They walk to the counter. Lindsay smashes half an avocado

into a bowl while Gabby touches the bright-colored wrappers of the chocolates, reads the labels, and sucks on one until it dissolves in her mouth.

"I thought you'd be getting a tan," Gabby says.

"I never let the sun get on my face," Lindsay answers, putting an organic white corn tortilla triangle loaded with pale green guacamole in her mouth.

Gabby nods, surprised at Lindsay's independence in an era when people pay to lie in hot brightly lit coffins to bake the life out of their skins.

Lindsay and Gabby are deciding where to eat when Peter arrives. Forty-three, tall, energetic, and strategically ingratiating, he has a high-powered publicity job at a major movie studio and parties with the stars. He went to art school in New York and began his career designing book covers. He sometimes sent the books to Lindsay. She didn't read them, but she liked to show them off. Gabby asked to keep the ones she particularly admired.

In high school, Peter and Gabby's brother, Geoffrey, an artistic duo, dressed their preadolescent sisters in futuristic costumes of surreal colors and asymmetrical shapes then arranged their bodies in abstract formations in public spaces. While Lindsay got distracted and wandered off, Gabby was fixed on pleasing them. Gabby's painted image signaling "SWERVE" in a series of flag semaphore poses on The Bridge of Auspicious Improbabilities remains on a downtown Los Angeles freeway wall. She longs for her life to be otherworldly again.

At Lindsay's evening wedding reception with its Triple Crown motif—fascinators and fedoras requested along with formal dress—Peter and Gabby—wearing paper headgear produced as a children's library art project—discussed the writers and illustrators they knew. They slow-danced to the country western band, hoping everyone was too drunk to notice the way they rubbed against each other and looked into each other's eyes. They made out in the parking lot, leaning against Gabby's car until Peter's parents came; then, Peter went with them.

Soon Peter moved back to Los Angeles. He took Gabby,

who rarely had a boyfriend, to rogue spots where he knew the maître d's and bouncers like The Subaltern and The Petting Zoo. Holding his hand, she followed close behind him. In his apartment decorated with framed book jackets and movie posters he had designed, they would begin kissing, unable to stop themselves.

In his bedroom they had sex beneath Geoffrey's painting *Escapar del Sueño—Escape from the Dream*—of Los Angeles washed up like laundry on the beach. Peter would talk about what Geoffrey would say if he could see them lying together until Peter felt guilty and went to watch TV, leaving Gabby alone. She didn't feel guilty. She didn't believe in doing anything she felt guilty about. When she came out and hung on Peter, lonely and frustrated, desperate for attention, he wouldn't touch her.

They decided not to do that anymore, but whenever they were thrown together—New Year's Eve, Fourth of July—the attraction remained. Peter was always seeing someone, but his relationships were increasingly short-lived, even though as he got older—his thin golden hair beginning to go, his skin beginning to sag, his face losing its shape—he wanted more and more to settle down. For Gabby, it was as if Geoffrey had returned, only more unavailable and indifferent to her pain.

"Come on. Let's go," Peter says, returning from the master bedroom where Gabby had him put his suitcase.

Peter's best friend from art school who now lives in Santa Barbara—Rob—and their dates are waiting at the bar in a hotel down the street, he explains.

Gabby and Lindsay look at each other. This doesn't sound like much of a treat for them, Gabby thinks.

She needs to brush her teeth and put some color on her face. "I have to go use my products," she says, thinking she's being terribly witty, thinking products are what this weekend is about, but Peter and Lindsay are talking and don't respond.

As they cruise the bar—Peter leading, Lindsay in gold lamé hip-huggers, Gabby in her librarian slacks and blouse—Gabby checks out the men. The one she thinks most attractive—silver-blond crewcut, metal-blue eyes, a fair English face, a wide brutish chest—is Rob.

Rob sits at a table with a black-haired woman in a black leather jacket on his lap, a petite hard-looking blonde across from them. They are all over forty, beginning to pucker toward the center and go limp at the edges. Gabby is surprised they dare go out, surprised the waiter serves them, it being Santa Barbara and all.

Peter orders and pays for a round of drinks. Lindsay sits by Peter and his blonde date and tries to participate in the conversation. They talk about movies. That is what they have in common. They all love movies, love keeping up with the gossip, which is one reason they like being around Peter.

Gabby sits on the edge and doesn't try to keep up. She watches Rob as he orders a plate of steamed asparagus. He offers everyone a piece. She smiles and shakes her head. No one takes one, so he eats them himself. Something is wrong with him, she thinks. There's something wrong in his life or he wouldn't be sucking down a plate of steamed asparagus at a bar; then, he paws at and kisses his date.

When the two couples get up to dance, Lindsay and Gabby excuse themselves. They are back at the apartment within an hour of leaving it, still wondering where to eat. They decide there's no point in including Peter in their plans for the weekend. Peter and Rob have arranged to play golf all day Saturday.

Lindsay is asleep in the guest bedroom, and Gabby is lying on the hide-a-bed in the living room reading when Peter comes in. She puts down her book as he sits in a chair near the foot of the mattress and tells her about his evening.

"This dating thing is costing me a fortune," he complains. After buying drinks for all of them, he bought dinner. In the morning he's taking Rob and the two women for brunch.

She nods sympathetically. He feels taken advantage of. She understands.

"So what's Rob's story?" she asks.

"Oh, jeez." He shakes his head.

Rob is married to a wonderful woman. They own an interior design business and have two teenage sons. Two years ago Rob met another woman. She was married with two kids. They carried on a long-distance relationship in Palm Springs. At the end of the most romantic weekend of their lives, they decided to give up everything and be together.

When Rob got home he received a call from the woman's husband. She was killed in a traffic accident. That night Rob disappeared. His wife kept calling Peter to find Rob. After six days Rob showed up. That was a year ago. Now he lives in a rooming house and sleeps on a mattress on the floor. He lost his license for driving under the influence. He can't decide whether to stay married or get divorced.

"That explains it," she says.

"Explains what?"

"Explains why he isn't quite all there. Haven't you noticed?"

He shrugs. "No. I guess I'm used to it."

Gabby's not surprised. Peter survives by ignoring many things.

"So that's why you wanted to come here for the weekend," she says.

"Yeah. I miss him. I used to stay with him and his wife all the time. Now I can't even talk to her because all she wants to do is talk about him."

He stands up, hanging over the bed like an angel waiting to be called upon or sent back.

"I thought you'd be out all night," she says as he comes toward her. She opens her arms, and he slips inside them. She holds her head to his chest and moves her hands inside the back of his shirt, his skin as familiar to her as her own. They kiss.

"I'm not going to do this," he says, stroking the back of her neck.

"Neither am I." She doesn't want the rejection that comes after she has sex with him. Besides, Lindsay's asleep in the next room. It wouldn't take much for her to come out and wonder what's going on.

They hold each other, she rubbing his back; then, he gets

up and goes to bed. She lies awake, feeling desire roll through her like the waves surging in and out on the dark empty shore.

The following afternoon Gabby accompanies Lindsay—wearing a sequin-studded rose-colored satin shirt from her line of cowgirl clothing—on what Lindsay calls a "Celebration of Avarice" house-and-garden tour to raise money for the indigent. While Lindsay discusses the black granite kitchen countertops with the homeowner who removed them at a bargain from a home he foreclosed, Gabby thinks of the similar jet slab of finality over Geoffrey's grave. On her eighteenth birthday, without consulting their parents, she arranged for his favorite word, "Mutability," to be carved above his name and dates.

For dinner Peter and Rob take Lindsay and Gabby to a sports bar. Over the televised cacophony of metal thunder sheets employed by a war-painted football crowd commemorating another season of domesticated violence, Lindsay enumerates her rescues of her four Jack Russell terriers.

Rob comments, "When I was gone so much, my wife and kids adopted a little dog. It barked every time I tried to pet it. It didn't matter what I did, that little dog didn't like me," and Gabby feels the dissonance of what it must have been like for him to live in his own home.

He turns to her. "Have you ever been married?"

"No," she responds, dismissing this potential commonality. "It never seemed like a viable plan."

In the bathroom, Lindsay says go for him.

Returning to the apartment in the back seat of Peter's car, Gabby listens to Rob's call from his sixteen-year-old ADHD son. Home alone, he needs a ride to a party. Rob can't help him.

Putting his phone away, Rob explains to Gabby he used to help his sons with their homework at night and drive them to school in the morning. Now he reads self-help books at night and breakfasts with a gang of guys at a diner.

She tells him that at her library the children help their parents who don't speak English, don't read and write, or don't know how to use computers. Often the teenagers work to support their families or take care of chronically ill relatives. One young man she helped apply for college had to drop out to care for his sister with sickle cell anemia while their mother was in the hospital.

"They don't expect to have parents who can help them," she says.

Rob takes her hand as he turns toward his window.

Eventually, she stands on the apartment balcony with him. Peter and Lindsay are in their bedrooms sleeping. Rob leans back against the railing, and she leans into him, his legs spread out, hers inside his, so as she stands on her tiptoes she can feel a glow where her pubic bone rubs against him. Her ears hum. The stars are like glitter sprinkled by a child onto black paper. Below them an Hispanic family comes from a wedding reception dressed in black tuxes and bright party dresses, still bubbling with festivity. Palm leaves rustle and sway in a cool breeze.

"This is paradise," he says. "I can't believe you don't come here all the time."

She shakes her head, afraid he'll lose interest if she explains the many reasons why she doesn't. They kiss, her body melting into his. She wants to pretend they are in paradise. She has not been there for a long time.

Finally, she pulls back and tells him she knows his story, knows what it is to lose the person you love since she lost her big brother when she was ten. She asks him where he went when he disappeared. He doesn't answer. She pictures him lying in a cave like Jesus Christ, a stone rolled across the entrance, his ghost rising to resume his responsibilities as her ghost has carried on for her.

"When my brother died, there was no one I could talk to," she says. "No one my age had lost anyone."

"I didn't know it could happen until I was over forty," he admits.

"It must be hard when you're that old." She can feel the shock of it.

"And it must be hard when you're that young," he replies with more compassion than she has ever gotten. She can see the concern on his face, hear it in his voice, and for a moment they are human again. What happened to them mattered. Their eyes cut through each other until their shells lie splintered around them like the husks of insects, and they have to look away.

He takes her hand as they go inside to lie on the hide-a-bed. She feels herself vibrating outside her body as her tongue touches the thin skin above his collarbone, as her fingers skim up and down his thigh, as her lips move over the blue veins of his groin. It is a miracle to her that she has charmed him. He wants to be with her more than he wants to be by himself or with someone else. And unlike her brother, he is not dead: Despite how fragile he is, he is alive. Instead of making love, they hold each other, hearts pressed together, as people after a tragedy do.

In the morning, when they arrive at his rooming house, he wants to know when he can see her again, as if they can keep the magic up, as if the complicated fabric now woven between them won't unravel into the tangles of everyday life.

She looks at his bright aristocratic face, thinks of the generations of good breeding behind it, and doesn't answer. He has a whole life here: the date from two nights before, his wife, his sons, his business. How can he know what this means to her? He can't. And after a few more times, she'll lose interest in him. It always happens. No one can understand her or divert her as her brother did.

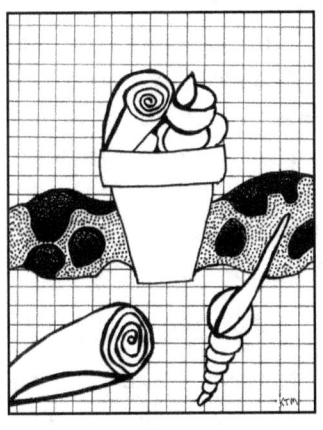

# of Chemistry and Geography

AT FORTY-EIGHT MY FRIEND Claire still has tawny shoulder-length hair; her blue eyes are still childlike and optimistic. She lives in my parents' apartment building near the beach in Santa Barbara. She arrived there from Dayton, Ohio. She got to Ohio from Virginia Beach where she lived as a child. Virginia Beach was quaint and safe, and she was happy there. But when Claire was a teenager, her father moved the family to Dayton. Life in Ohio seemed unreal to her. She longed to be in a small coastal town.

As a high school English teacher, she loved working with the disadvantaged kids in a bad section of the city, but after a few years vowed she would not die in Ohio. Leaving behind her parents, young sister, and secure career, she convinced a friend to drive her to California. Claire doesn't drive well. Arriving in Los Angeles, they headed up the coast looking for a place Claire could live.

When they pulled off the freeway north of Ventura, she knew she had found the place. They stayed at a bed and breakfast. Across the street was an apartment for rent. Claire has lived there ever since. What she likes best is to sit outside in her folding chair, read, and drink Coke. She would like a boyfriend, but since she prefers to stay home, she doesn't meet anyone.

Even though Claire loves Midwestern food—pork chops and mashed potatoes—she stays bikini thin by eating small portions

45

at dinner and drinking Cokes all day so she doesn't have to eat breakfast or lunch. She started drinking Cokes as a teenager. When she moved out of her parents' house, she realized she could drink as many as she wanted. When we go out for dinner, she orders two. As the icy tall glasses are lined up before her, her eyes and smile widen, and she presses her hands together in excitement.

It isn't the caffeine, she has informed me, because she has switched to caffeine-free. It is something else.

When she arrived, Claire taught at a private school, but the pay was too low to survive on. She didn't think she could get a job at a public school, so she let her teaching credential lapse. At a stone company she sold marble to Bo Derek and other stars; then, she marketed textbooks, traveling around the country to trade shows. At forty, she wanted a more stationary and meaningful career. She decided to become a nurse. Even though she isn't good at math or science and has no great physical ability, she is conscientious and cares about people. Most important, medical service is the largest industry in the area.

She worked as an aide in a prestigious clinic while her name moved up the list for the community college nursing program. She loved her work and her employers valued her. She made just enough to survive on if she didn't buy anything but groceries, gas, and Coke. After she got into the nursing program and had to leave her job, her greatest pride was that despite how poor she was, she still managed to afford California blonde hair, courtesy of the gay hairdresser she had a crush on, and Coke.

One November her mother died suddenly, and Claire went to Ohio for the funeral. As she looked at the frozen dreary land, she thought the worst thing in the world was to be buried somewhere you didn't belong. Despite her poverty and loneliness, she was more convinced than ever she had made the right decision. Her twin niece and nephew, toddlers, called her ever-present Coke her "juice," she told me when she got home. "Aunt Claire needs her juice," they'd say.

She knew her habit probably wasn't good for her. In nursing

school she learned that the phosphoric acid in carbonation interferes with the utilization of calcium in bones causing them to crumble. She explained the chemistry to me. She joked that this would happen to her when she got old. But she isn't that old, and it is happening now.

Not long ago Claire tripped in her living room and fell, shattering both arms—the humerus bones, two of the thickest bones in the body—just below her shoulders. She was glad she lived alone and no one had seen her fall, but when she tried to push herself up she couldn't. She thought she was paralyzed. She remembered her nurse's training and tested her fingers. They worked.

She forced herself up by her better arm. It hurt. Besides that, there was almost no pain. She edged onto her bed then walked to her phone, her arms swinging like elephant trunks. She called a friend who took her to the doctor who sent her to the hospital.

In the x-rays the top of one humerus looked like crushed corn flakes, the surgeon said as he decided how to put pins in it. Her bones had bled so badly her skin was black to her elbows. She almost required a transfusion. The doctor couldn't figure out how such a minor fall could cause such major damage to a person Claire's age. She couldn't understand it either, she said. She didn't tell him about the Cokes.

Luckily she had medical insurance from her former employer, the clinic. The doctors she had worked for visited her during the week she was in the hospital and made sure her care was the best. One doctor friend told her she wouldn't be able to drink Cokes any more then broke down and brought her a twelve-pack.

When Claire got back to her apartment, her retired father came from Ohio to take care of her. He bought her tent dresses with Velcro tabs and took her to dinner.

"He cut up my meat just like he used to do for the twins," she explained cheerfully.

She showed me her kitchen counters where everything was arranged so she didn't have to reach up or bend down. Hanging from a door knob was the large rubber band she stretched to build back the muscles in her arms. She took a calcium supplement so strong she had to stand for half an hour after she drank it so she wouldn't choke and die.

As we stood in the living room she hadn't been able to clean since she tripped, looking at the tropical view out the sliding glass doors, she remarked, "When my father was ready to go home, he wouldn't let me walk him to the bus stop. He was afraid I would fall. 'I couldn't help you then,' he said."

She used to walk to the store in the evenings and bring home two six-packs of Coke. Now she can't carry that much, so she goes to the motel across the street and gets two cans at a time from the vending machine. She wants to complete her nurse's training, but she doesn't know if she'll ever be strong enough to lift patients. She had planned to go into health education to teach people how to take care of themselves.

"I only wanted three things out of life," she said, "to live at the beach, to have blonde hair, and to be able to drink Cokes."

But the sun can give you cancer, bleach can ruin your hair, and soft drinks can cause your bones to decompose inside you.

Knowledge of
Material Limitations

CALLING ON SAINT CATHERINE OF Alexandria—the patron saint of those who work with a wheel— Natalie finally finished her MFA in ceramics and decided to flee the crowds piling up in her native California to teach at a small private college above a strip mine of a town in depressed rural central Ohio. The area was once famous for its pottery, so she went thinking she would find inspiration, free clay, and a free studio space.

Before she left San Francisco, her friends held her funeral. At sunset on a rocky strand called "Moaning Cove," the scruffy crew filled a black cardboard coffin with the papier-mâché mask she had made for a performance piece and the baton twirler's outfit she liked to wear out dancing. Sprinkling them with torn toll receipts from all the city's bridges, they chanted *"Kyrie eleison*: Lord, have mercy," while she placed pinwheel fireworks— symbolic of the spiked wheel of torture the Romans failed to execute Saint Catherine on—around the box and set them off.

Searching for the bucolic landscape of her childhood, this is what Natalie found: Parkersburg, West Virginia, which had whorehouses and moonshine, and Wheeling, which had the interstate and all the Rax family restaurants, Payless shoe outlets, and Sears shopping malls required to keep the impoverished residents going. Dying trees and rocky ground marked the mountainous northeast. To the west, dun-colored fields where no crops grew and no animals roamed were topped by twenty-foot-high metal pipe crosses, always in a pattern of three.

After settling in, she drove to the serpentine walls built thousands of years before by the Mound Builder Indians. What remained of the ceremonial earthworks was surrounded by suburban homes. Park swings and picnic tables were scattered among the disjointed humps. Half the mounds had been plowed under to erect the Mound Builder's Mall: "The Largest Mall in Central Ohio" a sign in an orange and brown Native American design proclaimed.

Looming over the hundred-and-fifty-year-old red brick campus was Lewis R. Browne, the college minister. Tall and broodingly handsome with an impressive prow-like nose, he was once a nuclear physicist for the Navy, running atomic submarines. Natalie figured he knew a lot about the power of God, and having served his time in darkness, he now seemed eager to serve in the light. The conservative students thought he was too liberal and the liberal ones thought he was too strange, but Thursday morning chapel was the highlight of her week. She longed for prayer, ritual, and passionate belief.

Reverend Browne had a beautiful voice, full of strength and authority. He talked about God, our Father, and how He was going to forgive us, and Jesus, His Son, and how He came to save us. Natalie kept hoping he'd mention some women in all this—it seemed so unnatural without any—and glancing around, she didn't see many sinners. All she saw were a few complacent country kids and the grayed adults who supervised them. She knew she hadn't found any opportunity to stray. She wished he'd tell them he was sorry they led such dull lives but keep it up.

Besides Reverend Browne, who was divorced, the only single person on campus near Natalie's age was Ruth, the librarian, who had grown up on a little farm nearby. Until she went to college she had never eaten a tomato or mayonnaise, she said.

In the cafeteria one day Natalie was trying to ignore the decor—orange plaid carpet, green Naugahyde booths and chairs, and brass five-point-star overhead lights—while separating her spareribs from the grease they reclined in when Reverend Browne passed by and waved.

Ruth leaned over her canned fruit cocktail and shredded lettuce brought from home to whisper, "It's worse than being a doctor or a lawyer sometimes, the things I find out about people by the books they read."

The minister read a lot about family psychology and sexuality, which was in his line of work, she supposed, but he also read about other religions: Buddhists and Muslims, Mayan prophecies, and Aztec sacrificial rites.

"If the college knew they were paying him to order books full of pictures of stone fertility goddesses, they'd get rid of him right now. He'd be better off drinking or messing around," Ruth said.

Natalie agreed. It sounded like he had potential.

While Saint Catherine had converted the pagan philosophers sent to debate her, Reverend Browne made himself useful by volunteering for everything from judging the annual talent show to organizing the intramural Olympics, Natalie observed. In one week she saw him at the women's volleyball game, the planning meeting for the Faith Union Christian Alcohol Awareness Day, and the local bar watching football with the guys. He walked a fine line to hold onto his job.

The day Ruth was at a "Color Me Beautiful" workshop, Natalie stood in the cafeteria holding her tray not knowing where to sit. Reverend Browne was at the coaches' table getting the scoop on the games. He looked at her and smiled. There was an empty seat, but he didn't nod or gesture to it. She walked toward it anyway then realized she'd be the only female and too nervous to choke down her dry shiny roast beef. She chose a vacant table.

When the coaches' table cleared, Reverend Browne stopped by, leaning down and bracing his large hands beside her.

"Why didn't you sit with us?" he asked.

"I figured if I couldn't enjoy the food, I could at least enjoy the company," she said, pointing to the empty chairs around her. "Besides, you could have invited me."

"Invited you?"

"Yeah," Natalie said not knowing if her suggestion was inappropriate. Saint Catherine had been beheaded for expressing her beliefs.

"You're never going to fit in if you don't try," he said.

Neither one of them was going to fit in no matter how hard they tried, she wanted to tell him.

"Maybe not," she said.

He shook his head and walked away.

At chapel Lewis gave a sermon called "Building Icons."

"I shall put no God before me!" he roared, slamming a twelve-inch television set down on the pulpit.

Two students in the first row jumped.

"I shall put no God before me!" He looked where there was a steady electronic hiss behind the podium. A remote-control car whirled across the stage.

"I shall put no God before me!" He shouldered a boom box and thrust up the volume so the chapel echoed with rock music.

Everyone eyeballed each other and him, but he didn't seem to notice. He turned on the TV again, powered up the car, boogied around the stage with the boom box going.

Saint Catherine was one to stir the pot a bit too, Natalie recalled.

Late Friday afternoon Lewis stopped by the art building while she unloaded clay she had dug up nearby.

"I liked your sermon," she said.

"No," he answered, shaking his head. "I got carried away."

He helped her haul the heavy plastic bags downstairs to her studio. She pointed to the open trench where the cement had been jackhammered away so the steam pipes could be repaired and the found sculpture she had made of broken desks and easels.

He was the first person here to see her work—pots bent and wrinkled under their own weight and pieces that had exploded in the kiln reassembled in new forms.

"I like to push the materials," she explained.

"Yeah," he responded.

He told her about the drumming ceremony he had gone to for the fall equinox and showed her an essay he had just gotten published about the pagan idols worshiped in the Old Testament. Finally, she said she had to go.

"Would you like to come to dinner?" he asked. He lived up the street. He was always having people over, and she had always wanted to go.

"Sure." It was the first invitation she'd had since she left San Francisco.

His house was dark and filled with assorted furniture—Danish modern, Oriental, teak—from his travels in the Navy.

They sat down and heaped their plates with green beans, meat loaf, mashed potatoes, and gravy.

"Aren't you going to say grace?" she asked.

"Grace," he said, arching one dark eyebrow at her; then, he started to eat.

Halfway through the meal he said he was going to Washington, D.C., the second week of December to visit friends.

"But that's the week of finals," she said.

"I know. I always leave during finals week," he answered.

"Don't the kids need someone to talk to then?"

"Yeah. That's why I go on vacation. That way I'm not around."

No wonder the kids don't like you, she almost replied. She didn't mind her job—the students were diligent and docile. It was the landscape she couldn't stand. Nothing relieved her desolation. She told him she was thinking of leaving at the end of the year.

"No," he said, looking serious and hurt.

She stared at him.

"If you have to go, I wish you luck. But I'll miss you," he answered.

She knew he meant it though they had failed to be anything for each other.

After they did the dishes, he invited her to watch a movie. He turned off all the lights but one, and they sat on the couch.

The movie was about a high school principal who sold his wife's jewelry to pay for prostitutes. When he got caught soliciting, he lost his job and none of their friends would speak to them, but because it was a movie, this brought the man and his wife closer together.

When it was over, Lewis jumped up and turned on the lights.

"I couldn't relate to that at all," he said standing in the center of the room.

"It reminds me of the town where I grew up," she replied.

He looked at her.

"The minister and the doctor wife-swapped. They even swapped kids. It was in 'Dear Abby.'"

"I don't want to hear about it." He stepped toward the front door, anxious for her to leave.

She stood and walked toward him. "Thanks for dinner," she said, reaching up to pat his shoulder.

He jumped back. As he opened the door, he didn't say "Goodnight" or "You're welcome."

Before she left the porch, he closed the door and turned off the light. She made her way down the dark winding path, touching the overgrown bushes. She felt punished, like she had stolen something.

On Monday, the head of the counseling center told her Lewis had come to the college after being caught with a married woman from his congregation. He lost his job as a minister in the largest Methodist church in D.C. His wife divorced him over it. The administration knew but liked his credentials and hired him anyway.

Sunday afternoon a few weeks later, Natalie was in Columbus, the nearest big city, when all the galleries downtown were having their openings. There were jugglers and musicians on the street, people selling food and handing out fliers. She wasn't too surprised to see Lewis with an attractive woman dressed like they had just come from church. She was surprised when he came over and asked how she was.

After he introduced her to Linda, the three went inside an

art installation—a big room resembling an ornate cathedral with dark blue gold-starred fabric on the walls and ceiling and big white candles dripping and smoking on pedestals and on an altar against the back wall.

"It looks like the stations of the cross," Natalie said.

They walked around examining each station. There were weird tobacco store sculptures of Aunt Jemima heads, black jockeys, and African voodoo dolls. In each was a slot to put a penny. A red light came on at the eyes or in the mouth of the figures, and pretty little music box tunes played like "Do, Re, Mi" from *The Sound of Music* and "On the Street Where You Live" from *My Fair Lady*. Natalie was spellbound by the smell of incense, the red lights, the candles, the tinkling harpsichord and chord organ music, and the formal primitive idea of the whole thing.

When they got to the door and could see that outside it was bright and normal, people were chatting and eating, Linda wanted to leave, but Natalie didn't. Lewis walked Linda outside then came back. Natalie asked him for more pennies, got out all the ones she had, and went from slot to slot playing all the tunes at once until they ran together like crazy ropes tugging at her.

"Doesn't it remind you of church?" she said. "Isn't this what church is supposed to be like?" She thought he would say yes, follow her analogy, try to better it as he always did, but he didn't say anything.

With a lot of hope and enthusiasm, she began. "Well, in church there's the choir singing in their robes, the organ music, the carvings and banners, the stained glass, the altar and all the things on it, even the minister's vestments. It's like theater, it's like an art piece, only from another time. Those things used to *mean* something."

He looked at her like she was saying something terrible until she realized she probably was.

"Don't take me so seriously," she said, but it was too late. He did take her seriously. She was the one playing around, trying to make him into something he wasn't.

Thursday morning she almost didn't go to chapel, but out of habit, because she was bored and didn't know what else to do, she went. Who was she to criticize Lewis? With all his contradictions, he was managing better than she was: "Do not sit in judgment, but rejoice in everything," Saint Catherine of Sienna had said.

For the sermon, Lewis had invited a woman to lead them whose ministry was dance. They stood in a circle near the altar acting out their emotions to the rhythm of her tambourine. She told the story of Job—his delight with his children, his flocks, and his prosperous farmland, then his acceptance of losing all he had. Natalie thought of her old life in San Francisco and her disappointment with her new life in Ohio.

When Job was further tested—his body covered with boils—he cursed his birth. Natalie followed the others as they shook their fingers at the innocent sky then cringed and begged God to answer them.

Like Job's friends who blamed his fate on his hidden sins, Natalie and Lewis pursued one another, fingers arched into hooks, teeth bared, moving through the others as if they were pillars of salt. When God responded to Job from the whirlwind, Natalie and Lewis spun and wove around those repenting for having doubted Him.

Imitating God, who gave Job twice as much as he had before, Lewis made gestures of largess toward his congregation, but Natalie couldn't act it out. She didn't think the universe's accounting was that superficial. Job had glimpsed the omnipotence of the Creator, but the emphasis seemed to be on how much stuff he got.

While the tambourine jangled in exaltation, she turned to the sunlight shimmering down from the rose window high in the chapel loft. Transfixed by its numinous radiance, her condemnations momentarily ceased.

Big Mama's

GROUP IS FINALLY OVER, THANK God. I'm lying on the floor in my room here at Big Mama's, this home for misfit wards of Ohio, doing these drawings with a protractor and colored pencils I found in the attic. For once it's quiet, and I can breathe.

Tonight David, our therapist, made us share our experiences with positive feedback. Like we had any. People shared the most ridiculous crap, like someone saying "Thank you" to them in the grocery store. David's new. He's the only man who comes around, so everyone's sucking up to him so he won't leave like our fathers always did. David made us think of one nice thing to say about the person next to us. Luckily, I was sitting next to my friend Ricky, or it would have been impossible. I said Ricky is a good listener, which he is. That's unusual around here. He can actually pay attention to someone.

When I first came, we were playing poker in the kitchen one night. Ricky stopped the game and made everyone put their hands down on the table—very strange—then he told us to turn them over, palms up. I looked at him.

"You too," he said.

So I put my palms up like everyone else's except across my wrists are these raggedy-looking scars. I did it with a broken beer bottle.

"Are those what I think they are?" he said, sounding real concerned.

I nodded.

"Okay," he said, and he told us to put our arms down.

I call it "Big Mama's" since all these women run the show. To keep this big Victorian from being bulldozed, some Cleveland socialite got her friends to donate to this worthy cause. There's ten of us, girls and boys, an experiment in family living. Everybody knows it's not working, but until somebody gets raped or beaten up, we're supposed to be grateful.

I'm here because my mom drinks and won't stop my big brother from pounding on me. She used to be jealous if my father paid any attention to me. After he left, she was on my brother all the time—wouldn't let him date or drive the car or get a job. He just had to be home. Then she started doing creepy stuff like opening the shower door when he was in there and talking about his private parts. My brother started taking it out on me because I could come and go as I pleased. One time he slammed my head into the front door knob. The extension part just missed my eye. Another time he hit me in the face with the telephone, one of those big old-fashioned black dial kind. Now my brother's alone with my mom. I worry about him.

My roommate, Laura, is spending the night with her grandparents even though it's against the rules to miss group. Laura's grandparents are rich and give a lot of money to this place, so she can do what she wants. The other kids are jealous. I was, too, but her life's as messed up as any of ours. Her mom was a debutante, but she went through this rebellious phase and served her kids road kill and got committed. "Pain is pain," Laura says. She's right. Sometimes it seems like there's so much pain in this house, the whole place is going to collapse; then, more comes in the door and the house still stands. That's those Victorians for you.

The drawings are for cards, in case I ever want to write anybody, like my pen pal in prison or my father or my mom. I like using the protractor because it sets the circles straight. A lot of kids here live like slobs, some kind of reaction to their environment, but Laura and I like everything neat. That's why we get along. It doesn't hurt she's gone most of the time too.

Oh yeah, the other reason we're here is because we're gifted. Good thinking—put together ten teenaged fucked-up kids with egos the size of mushroom clouds, a couple of overworked neurotic surrogate mothers, and a counselor guy who drops by once a week to do research for his master's. That's your basic American family, all right. Murderous and suicidal to the core. "Murderous" is a big word around here. We're all supposed to get in touch with our "murderous rage" without acting on it. Sort of like giving little kids matches and dynamite and telling them not to start a fire.

I'm having a pretty good time for once in my life doing these designs until I hear Jules, he's one of the boys, and Leticia, she's the housekeeper, fucking—slam, slam, slam—in Leticia's room next door. She's nineteen and black and getting fat already. I think she missed her opportunity to be one of us, and now she's making up for it. The boys have the third floor, and you have to be in your own room after eleven o'clock—that's lights out—but you can do a lot of fucking before eleven, especially when Dorothy's here. She's the night aide. She's got an umbilical cord from her head to the TV and never hears a thing.

The springs make me sick, the way they creak. I feel like someone's doing it to me. Jules grunts like a pig: "*Uhh. Uhh. Uhh.*" He's this little guy with almond skin and kinky hair.

Leticia moans: "*Ohh. Ohh.*" Better her than me, that's all I've got to say. She says she and Jules are engaged. She's got a ring, but I think she bought it. No one's supposed to know they're together, but everybody does, just like with everything around here.

I almost did it with Jules once, but he reminds me of my brother, the way they both smile real cute and show off, and it gave me the creeps. When I told him no, he said, "I'll *kill* you." Now I'm scared of him. His mother was white—blonde, like me. His dad was black. His mom ran away when he was five. Left him with his dad and grandmother. They both drank. Jules started stealing so they'd have enough to eat. Jules has this thing about white women. He doesn't like it when they leave him.

Whenever I walk into a room, he looks at me like how do

I dare be alive. My stomach cramps up and I try to get out. If I have to sit near him at meals, I can't eat, no matter how hungry I am. Jules usually says something smart like "Oh, she's feeling *delicate* again." Like anybody dares to feel delicate around here.

Ricky says not to worry about Jules, but Ricky gets along with everybody. Jules isn't a real powerhouse, but he's a juvenile delinquent for Christ's sake. He's done bad stuff—setting cats on fire and even burglaries. He knows how to get in locked windows and doors. I've seen him do it. I'm scared all the time that he'll break into my room when I'm gone and burn my drawings or my writing.

Leticia's bed is still banging the wall. You'd think they'd at least put the mattress on the floor like Ricky and Isabelle do, but that's way too polite for Jules. Why bother if he can't make a scene. And now they've got the music going too. Jazz. I hate jazz. It reminds me of being stuck in traffic—horns blowing and everybody shouting.

Next door I hear Ricky and Isabelle in her room. They talk real low, cooing at each other. It makes me sick. "Why don't you coo at me?" I want to say to Ricky. He'd look at me like I was crazy. Ricky's here because his mother's dead. His father date-raped his mom when she was fifteen. He was the result. His father told him how he planned the rape. His father's a sex therapist. His mother blamed Ricky for ruining her life. He says she looked like Glenda, the Good Witch. Everyone in his family is tall and fair. He's small and dark.

One time I went into his room without knocking. He was putting fingernail polish on his big toe. He was real embarrassed. It was his mom's polish. He'd saved it. He was missing her. I sat down beside him and felt sad. He saves everything. He's even got a box for the stuff I give him. He's the only one here who can stand to listen to anyone else, but he's usually drunk. In the evenings, after dinner, when no one notices, he drinks Sloe Gin and makes out with Isabelle or plays piano or paints.

I'm getting so freaked out listening to Jules and Leticia slamming and Ricky and Isabelle cooing that I can't draw. I turn over and look at my hands in the air, quivering. My stomach feels like a bomb exploded in it. I could go down and complain. We've got this big rule—no noise after seven. But I know it won't get me anywhere, like at home. After my brother tried to plant the telephone in my face, my mother started arguing with him about what his problem was. I was the one sitting there bleeding.

We're supposed to be doing our homework and improving our minds. That's fine by me. I'd love to improve my mind, but I don't seem to be able to. I'd like to go talk to Ricky, but Isabelle's this insecure bitch. He's always protecting her, so he won't talk to me when she's around, like I'm this numb nuts and can take it, or like I don't count.

I hate Isabelle because she's this absolute twit. I mean, I want to hit her or something, wake her up. But that's why she's here. She got beat up all the time by her dad. I guess what really makes me mad is she's some prima donna poet. Frieda, she's the head Big Mama, loves Isabelle's writing. All the little old ladies who run this place do too. They're all the time arranging for her to read her poetry at their little old lady things. I think it's real rude, her and me both being poets, and she gets to go out and I don't. I've written over a thousand poems. I get them published all the time in the school newspaper. I gave some to Frieda, but she never said anything about them. I don't think she read them.

I complained to Frieda about Isabelle once. Frieda said what everybody says, "Life sucks." Actually, she wasn't that sympathetic. She went on about how I'd just have to understand that Isabelle had some major gift for sucking up to little old ladies. No, that's what I wish she'd said. What she said was that not everyone can be as talented as Isabelle, and I'd just have to realize that, and Isabelle's talent was a burden to bear, and all that she's-so-sensitive crap.

Maybe if I walked around like an S-curve like she does, her head all bowed over, people would be nice to me too, but it's not my style. I walk around more like an I-beam. Everyone thinks I'm some ad for Samsonite luggage, like I can fall off a ten-story building then have some ape jump on me and it doesn't hurt.

Like today. After school I was waiting in line to get on the bus, and Jules was ahead of me. He stuck his tongue out at me with this big wad of drool on it. Everybody laughed, and he put his tongue in. Just as the line started moving and everyone was looking toward the bus, he turned around, puckered up his lips with all this hate and disgust, and spit on me like in some sleazeball gangster movie.

I just stood there wiping my face while everyone else got on the bus. I climbed up in time to see Jules walking down the aisle all pigeon-toed with his butt sticking out saying "Hi" real cute to everybody, everybody saying "Hi" real friendly back to him. I sat in the first empty seat I found, like a machine.

When I got home I went to tell Frieda, but my timing was bad, as usual. With Frieda, everything I do sucks. It's all I can do not to call her "cunt" to her face. People think she's nice because she smiles all the time, but it's this eat-me-then-die smile. She got knocked up in college, and she hasn't gotten over it yet. Her daughter's in college now.

When I first got here and saw how sweetie-pie Frieda was to everyone, I thought maybe she'd be sweetie-pie to me too. I'd offer to do things for her, get her coffee or straighten up like I'd do for my mom, but it always seemed like I was bugging Frieda. It took me a while to notice everyone was sucking up to her, and they're all better at it than I am. Jules is always rubbing his head against her shoulder and acting dopey around her. She lets him.

Anyway, when I went to tell on Jules, hoping Frieda would maybe make him stay in his room, or at least apologize, Jules was already in her office showing her some drawing he did, his feet crossed and swinging because they won't reach the floor, his head wagging, and this Howdy-Doody grin on his face. I told Frieda I'd come back later. She said fine.

So when I did, it was almost time for her to go home. She had this stack of stuff on her desk she was working on. She's always complaining about being overworked. All day she sits in the common room talking to whoever's there about all her problems then being so sympathetic about all their problems;

then, when she gets back to her office and sees all the stuff on her desk, she blows up. So I told her I had a problem, and she said "What?" real pissed off already.

"Jules spit on me," I said. I wanted to laugh because it sounded so stupid, but I was trying to keep serious because I felt my rights had been infringed on.

"Christ," she said. "What do you want me to do about it?"

"You could make him apologize. You could ground him. I thought we were supposed to be socialized around here. I thought you'd want to know."

"I don't have time for this!" she yelled. She pointed her finger at her desk. "I've got work to do. The trustees are coming tomorrow. They expect these records to be up to date. You straighten it out!"

She walked out and left me standing there. I went and stood in the common room for a while. Frieda came back through.

"I'm sorry, Frieda," I said, like a fool. "I thought you ought to know."

"I'm sick of this place," she said. "I can't keep up with all of you. I don't have time for everyone's little complaints. You'll just have to learn to get along."

She went back into her office and slammed the door. I stood there for a while, getting more pissed off. I mean, how inappropriate could she be? All my life I've been trying to get along with people who want to either fuck me or kill me. People keep telling me there's a way. Finally, I went outside and bounced a basketball against a wall for about an hour until I calmed down; then, I had to go to group and think of one nice thing to say.

It's after nine and I'd like to sleep, but Jules and Leticia still have the music on. I reach over and knock on the wall. Her bedsprings creak, and Jules turns the music up louder. I'm scared to knock on the door, not that he's likely to turn the music down or do anything I ask him. I'm going to have to get Dorothy. She's like this manic-depressive paranoid schizophrenic. If it's quiet for one fucking minute she hears burglars and rapists and people talking about her and gets lonely and loses touch with reality and all this really extreme stuff just because her father tried to get into her pants a few times. She's almost forty, and she still makes him pay her car insurance and give her money like some prostitute. I hope I have it more together by the time I'm forty.

She sits in the common room wrapped in blankets with the lights on, the TV going, a radio going, a couple of alarm clocks going off all the time to remind her to take her pills and call her mother and go to the bathroom or whatever she does. She writes protest letters to Congress and letters to the editor and letters to Santa Claus, I guess, making all these piles of garbage around her. She's always trying to get us to write letters or sign letters, and we have to keep telling her we're too busy and we're not old enough to vote and all that. She gets real hysterical and begs us to fight for our rights. She's definitely a mess.

I go downstairs. I stand in front of the TV and tell Dorothy I'm not moving until she tells Leticia and Jules to knock it off. She heaves herself up and follows me upstairs. I go to my room. She goes to Leticia's room. Her and Jules and Leticia start talking and laughing. I'm in my bed listening to this. I'm so pissed off my stomach cramps up. I put the pillow over my head, but I can't stand it.

"Shut up!" I scream. "Shut the fuck up! I'm trying to sleep!"

It does get quiet next door; then, Dorothy comes in. She tells me she's going to have to write me up.

"No way," I say.

"It's the rules," she says.

I could kill her. She turns my light out and goes back downstairs. I get up and turn the light back on. I'm wide awake again.

In the morning I'm fried out of my mind, naturally, having gotten about four hours sleep. At breakfast I notice on the checkoff sheet that Dorothy wrote me up for making noise during quiet hours, yelling at her, and having my light on. She wrote Jules up for exactly nothing. And there's Leticia doing the dishes, humming. I hear Jules jumping down the stairs, his feet together like some little kid, and my stomach knots up.

He comes in. He says to Leticia in this fake charming voice, "How's my little mama," and hugs her from behind, burying his hair in her neck while she giggles. He turns his head and sticks out his tongue at me. I flip him off.

Frieda comes in. Make my day a total nightmare. Jules pours her coffee and gets her cream and sugar like she's Lady Di coming to visit; then, he tells her about some art project he's working on. Frieda's all smiley-faced and cow-eyed. It's classic.

I shove myself away from the table, making the silverware bounce. I was starving, but now I'm too pissed off to eat. I go upstairs, brush my teeth, and get the hell out. I put my shoes on waiting for the bus, thinking what an excellent day this has been already.

When I get home from school, Frieda calls me into her office. She says Jules told her I was playing Laura's stereo real loud during quiet hours and he had to get Dorothy to shut me up, so now I'm grounded for two weeks.

For some unknown reason I totally lose it and start shouting, "That's bullshit! Jules had the stereo blasting! I complained about him!"

"That's not what Dorothy's report says."

"Dorothy's a goddamn liar. She's covering up for him!"

"I will not tolerate this screaming!" Frieda screams. "I don't know what the hell goes on when I'm not here. I can't be gone for five minutes! I'm sick of this! You go to your room right now before I have you put in juvenile hall!"

I go to my room. I'm crying. On the floor are the drawings I made last night. I remember how happy I was making them and how quiet it was when I first started. I reach over and scrape them up, twist them as tight as I can. I start shredding them, all the soft colors torn to bits. I'm crying so hard I can't stand up. I flop on my bed and pound it with my fist. If I get caught I'll be in even bigger trouble, but I can't stop. I pound my head against the wall. I expect to hear Frieda, but she doesn't come up. After a while my head hurts, so I stop. I'm not crying any more, and pretty soon I fall asleep.

When I wake up, Laura's home. She's working at her desk.

"Hi," she says.

She's picked up my drawings and thrown them away. The room looks real clean and neat, like nothing has happened, and so I guess nothing has.

Subvert-Yr-Cat

WHEN ANNA GETS HOME FROM her job doing PR for a large and profitable hospital, she runs four miles, microwaves a frozen dinner, eats, then draws storyboards for commercials. She makes up the products such as Subvert-Yr-Cat, patterned after a popular cat food: "Feed your cat Subvert-Yr-Cat for a leaner, meaner, more covert cat. Turn your proper aristocratic pet into an information retrieval system. Simply feed as usual. Your cat will be able to infiltrate and observe radical groups, disseminate disinformation, and report back to you! No prescription necessary. Available wherever fine pet foods are sold."

Why is she doing this? It's getting her nowhere. It's not even part of a tradition, like diary writing; however, people do look forward to seeing her drawings in the newsletter she's responsible for producing at work. She runs four miles because she does triathlons, badly.

After graduating from The Ohio State University in visual communication design where she excelled in usability testing, she applied for a PR job in the bombed-out heart of Peoria. When she went for the interview, she got the impression World War III had taken place, and we had lost. Believing that as an educated person she could make real choices about her lifestyle, she said to herself, *I could never live in a place like this,* and refused the job. It was six months before she got a worse job for less pay in an Ohio town that once thought of itself as the western frontier; now, the unemployed residents sit on their front porches, lost. When her status-conscious parents visited her, she had to explain she was not responsible for the economic situation that created the circumstances of her life. Her mother, a Republican, accused her of being a dyed-in-the-wool Democrat.

By expressing an interest in her community, Anna has learned that in her county eleven thousand people cannot read. When she asked a co-worker to measure something, the young woman, a graduate from a local college, protested that she didn't know how to use a ruler, as if it were a complicated piece of equipment requiring training to employ. Welfare is the second-largest industry here, after hospitals, of which there are two, thus prompting the need for a PR department with a specialization in graphic illustration, which Anna has. The welfare department just spent three million dollars building itself a new office, her landlord told her, to handle poverty in more gracious surroundings. Because she lives in the vacated downtown neighborhood that has the highest incidence of crime and poverty in the city, Anna is beginning to appreciate the desire for more gracious surroundings, as her parents hoped she would. "Where Have All the Flowers Gone?" she sings when she jogs through the hot humid downtown at night that smells of urine, beer, and rot and past the river too polluted to swim in.

Anna is lying on her couch, incapable of moving, having run six instead of her usual four miles at a ten-second-faster pace. It is 8 p.m. At 5:30 a.m., she will get up to swim. Because of all her training, she is constantly hungry and thirsty, tired and having to pee. When people admire her hard work and dedication, she finds it embarrassing. She thinks it is a bad sign that her narcissistic ability to create and meet so many needs for herself receives so much approval.

As she eats from a box of chemical-yellow cheese crackers, she reads the label. It says "Hundreds of uses." What are you supposed to do with them, use the hole in the center to hang them on your Christmas tree? Or perhaps string them, with popcorn, for a necklace? The only thing you can really do with them is eat them, so how can they say "Hundreds of uses"?

Where's the truth in that? She learned in a consumer rights workshop that to make such statements is against the law. Where is the disclaimer? The availability of lab reports and statistical research?

Anna rechecks the box. It says "Hundreds of ways to enjoy them." Is "enjoy" the same as "use," or is she wrong? This is just the sort of thing people accuse her of doing all the time, taking something perfectly normal and twisting it to be quite a different thing, and always something more upsetting rather than something more pleasant. But why would she do that? Why would anyone? Yet, here again, apparently she has done it though she can't think of hundreds of ways to "enjoy" little chemical-yellow crackers either.

At twenty-three, she is tired of being a misunderstood adolescent. She thinks someone should understand her by now. Where is her "lifestyle enclave" as one sociologist termed a group of like-minded adults who choose to live in proximity to each other? Most of her neighbors are making their first voyages into the world after graduating from high school. At their gatherings they like to burn the arms and legs off their plastic deck furniture as evidenced by the debris left in the morning along with beer bottles and, yes, chemical-yellow cheese crackers and curls of corn. She would thrill to the luxury of having her private opinions echoed all around her, of coming home at night from her job at the hospital to see her street lined with neighbors carrying placards: "Truth in advertising! Recall chemical-yellow cheese crackers!" But no.

It seems to Anna this is just where all the trouble begins, and trouble certainly resounds these days. First, some boss tells some kid just out of college, "We want to promote these little yellow cheese crackers. There must be hundreds of uses for them. Find some."

The kid, who majored in art and minored in philosophy whose older brother is a corporate lawyer and brings beautiful women to family picnics in a metallic blue BMW while the kid comes with his parents in their faded white minivan, tastes one of these chemical-yellow salt-encrusted health hazards. He hasn't eaten food like this since he gave up Ding-Dongs and potato chips his freshman year of college. The crackers are yellow-orange like his Day-Glo tennis shoes back home in the closet, and artificial coloring isn't even mentioned in the ingredients. "Real cheese," it says. From what, a radioactive cow?

And now he has to find "hundreds of uses." At his computer, the kid asks for more information about the product. It comes up. He types in "Grind them in your blender for a super-absorbent low-weight high-impact creative culinary enhancement."

The screen flashes back at him: "Exceeds maximum word limit for this commercial application as specified by product producer."

He deletes "super-absorbent" and "low-weight." The computer accepts the slogan now, but he isn't getting anywhere. He asks for more boxes of the cracker-product and distributes them to the secretaries and anyone who will eat them, asking each person to put down in writing three uses for the item by the end of the day.

When he tallies the slips of paper, half the people have commented on taste or color instead of function. The other half have suggested only one use, which is eating them. That night he is distraught. He takes more boxes of the cracker-product home. He calls his mom, his big brother, makes his brother ask his date for possible uses for cheese crackers, consults with his brother on his legal and ethical responsibilities regarding these proposals.

A week later the kid throws in the towel, takes the project back to his boss, shows him all the research and the five most plausible uses, but admits he has no campaign, no slogan.

The boss grabs the pen out of the kid's shirt pocket, marks on one of the kid's drawings, shoves it back in his face. "Here. 'Hundreds of ways to enjoy these fine crackers.' That's it. See? Get it?"

"But, sir," the kid says, staring up at his boss.

The old guy pats him on the back and tells him to finish the ad and get it in by the end of the day.

That's just how the trouble begins, Anna is sure.

This is just the sort of thing that keeps happening. While eating the crackers, Anna looks through her mail. There is a postcard from Madeline, the wife of Anna's former doctor. Madeline, after graduating from law school in her native country, Sweden, and learning several foreign languages, became the Swedish equivalent of a CIA agent/spy; then, she married the doctor and spent the next thirty years as the secretary/janitor in his tiny office, paying bills, collecting money, straightening the examining rooms, etc., until the doctor died. Anna sent her a condolence note. A year went by. Now Anna holds her response, written from Sweden: "I am spending the summer here. It is great to see friends and family. I am doing several volunteer jobs. Things will never be the same and there is no future, but one gets used to this life. All the best. . . . "

Anna feels the same way. There is no future, but one gets used to this life. It is like an hourglass that has run down. There are no words to express how empty it is, and there is no way to get outside it to turn it over and make it run its course again. It's too boring to simply watch it—it's not going to fill itself—so you go about your business as all around you people say how empty and meaningless life is.

Anna thinks if they would just decide on what it means it would stop being meaningless. She was planning a special New Age edition of the newsletter and wanted to write an article for it entitled "Vegetable Ethics" in which she would argue that, as Georgia O'Keeffe said, "Life is meant to be lively. If making art makes your life lively then by all means make art," meaning life is like a plant, a growing thing, whose only true nature is to grow; then, Anna read not one but two books putting down the self-centeredness of her generation, accusing them of having nothing more than "vegetable ethics" in which life is like a growing plant and the highest good is what made the individual plant grow.

She decides to write an article on uses for chemical-yellow cheese crackers, part of her series about interesting ways to use food, like plastic resin-coated Twinkie doorstops and dried flower arrangements anchored in raw beans and brown rice. And she plans another ad. It is for Kitty on the Go, a freeze-dried reconstitutable cat: "Perfect for travelers, invalids, college students, and apartment dwellers. Simply add air and water any time you need a portable pet." After inventing it, she feels downhearted when she realizes it doesn't exist. She would like to have one.

The next morning she is in the pool before six for geriatric swimming as she calls it. She is the youngest person in the water by about forty years. The ladies say she is an inspiration because she swims so fast. She thinks they are an inspiration because they are so old and swim so slowly. They smile at each other a lot and tell each other to have a nice day when they are done. She eats a peanut butter and jelly sandwich in the car on the way to work and pours thick globs of yogurt down her throat from a container, a difficult maneuver in morning traffic.

At the coffee break she buys an influential liberal magazine instead of coffee because she has sworn off both caffeine and intellectual naïveté. She takes the magazine with her on a stroll around the halls, gathering more ideas for the New Age newsletter. The doctors smile and wave. They think she is doing a fine job. They like the cartoons of themselves in the newsletter. Anna goes into the nurses' lounge and listens to the nurses, who are all God-fearing and married, talk about grocery bills and house payments. She knows now what the politicians want when they say they want a return to traditional family values. They want people to feel so strapped they will do anything to hold on to their jobs.

According to everything she hears, which is quite a lot since her job in PR puts her in touch with so many people, everyone knows there is much wrong with modern life, but no one seems to know what to do about it, though some people believe if we all did something, like help build a low-income house or adopt a hard-to-place child or pick up the tab for somebody's major medical care, things would get taken care of.

This is not the Big Answer that Anna is looking for, but her peers are tired of her search for the Big Answer and would rather talk about their athletic training regimens, so they do.

They are more impressed when Anna tells them she runs nine-minute miles than when she tells them about the environmental threat of surface development encroachment. They are more interested in hearing about the latest bike path extension than hearing about the evolutionary flaw in the human brain that blocks neurological communication—endowing the entire species with schizophrenia.

It doesn't help that this is just a Sign of the Times, or that this is a Sign of the Times and it is a Bad Sign, or to ask the Big Question about how to turn this all around because the Big Question will lead to the Big Answer, a topic on which she will be silenced in favor of a return to the subject of Miles Covered Per Day, the principle concern of the triathletes she fraternizes with—the attractive articulate energetic young people whom she should perceive as her lifestyle enclave but does not.

On a Friday night before a competition she finds herself watching the Tour de France with her pseudo-companions from the triathlon club, an organization she resisted joining because its members exhibit athletic focus and ability superior to hers. There's a group of them spread out on a couple of couches in front of someone's wide-screen television drinking soda and beer and eating, yes, again, chemical-yellow crackers and corn curls.

Anna realizes that one of the group, Ian, a dedicated cyclist, is the prototype of the kid she calls up in her fantasies of how the young must be corrupted to get ahead, but Ian is beyond corruption. He works at a bike shop and probably has never entertained a fantasy of getting ahead except in a race. Anna wonders now, as the cyclists pump and sweat in a dangerous tight pack before them, if she has a crush on Ian. She decides she does. It will make the race more exciting though watching the Tour de France in a room full of triathletes is already heady stuff. Their identification with the stars is great since they train, race, and crash in similar, though less spectacular, ways.

As the cyclists sweat through hill after hill the announcer repeats clichés like "Man against mountain" and "Triumph over tragedy."

"'Give me liberty or give me death,'" Anna adds, but no one laughs. They are too intent on the bike race. Ian smiles at her over his bowl of cheese crackers though.

"It's from the *Communist Manifesto*," she whispers reassuringly.

They show out-takes of previous races. The leader of a pack falling and the entire pack crashing over and around him. Three cyclists going over the side of the Alps then being dragged out on stretchers. A monument to a biker, who twenty years ago, at one-hundred-fifty-degree ground temperatures, collapsed, was put back on his bike per his request, and died. The announcers mourn the loss of the great cyclist.

"Too bad the starving people in Africa don't have bicycles to die on so they can get their names on plaques," Anna says. No response.

Afterward, everyone goes home to bed because tomorrow they will be competing. Anna can't sleep and draws another commercial. This one is for Temper Tamper, a pill to help improve or restore defective parts of your personality like calcium tablets improve bones. Finally, around midnight, five hours before she has to be up, she falls asleep with her drawing pad and pencil in her hands. She dreams she is coaching the people she is going to the race with, which is awkward because they are serious competitors, and she is not. She exhausts herself trying to tell them what they already know.

In the morning, during the drive, Anna has nothing to say and tries to sleep. Occasionally, she hears her training mates talk about new running shoes or trisuits or glue to hold their tires to their rims. Their degree of expertise and the way they pass information around fascinate her. If they were all working on the Big Answer, she is sure they could combine the laws of motion, economics, and human motivation into an elegant solution, which is why she encourages them to do this even though they refuse.

She is nervous before the race starts, not because she feels pressured to succeed, but because fear is a normal reaction to the threat of pain. Anna apologizes to her traveling companions in advance for holding them up since they will have to wait a couple of hours after their races are done for her to finish. She asks herself why she is doing this then realizes it is probably healthier than staying home drawing incorrigibly ironic commercials advertising life as she sees it. She is embarrassed to be stretching with the real competitors—everyone else—and so compromises between pretending to stretch and pretending not to care. When her heat finally goes, she doubts she has laid out the right biking and running apparel, but she is committed now.

The swim is in a pool, so it is easy and safe. The only opportunity for injury comes at the end when she must pull herself onto the deck. There she skins her knee and her ankle, but not badly, though as the blood stains her socks she again appears to be more serious than she wants to appear. She has a rough time in the transition area, unable to get her shoes clipped into the pedals and her bike into the right gear, but finally, she is on the road.

They are in hilly Appalachian country. The route is steep and dangerous. There is no edge to ride on. People passing in cars honk and shout as they speed by. Anna flips them off. They go through a one-lane tunnel, over a newly tarred road with "Warning: Loose Gravel" signs, and dodge potholes until her shoes pop out of the clips so that going down a lumpy pitted hill at twenty-five miles an hour she loses her main source of stability and control.

Still working to get her shoes clipped in, she hits two sets of railroad tracks angled across the road. On the second set, her front tire catches in the tracks, and she is thrown from the bike, landing first on the side of her head then on the point of her left shoulder with a sickening soft crunch. Her shoulder and head seemed pinned to the asphalt. She is afraid to move them. She has never seen her shoulder from quite this angle. She imagines it is a Bad Sign.

All the time she thinks *This must be a mistake. I'm not really competing. I was just experimenting with a lifestyle.* The other cyclists whiz around her. Though she can't get up, she finds a way to lie back more comfortably on the ground. It is clear something real has occurred.

Soon a race official appears and takes her to the hospital for x-rays. She has a broken collarbone and a slight concussion. She is back at the race site about two hours after her comrades are, just as she predicted. On the ride home she is not interested in convincing anyone of the importance of anything. She just grits her teeth every time the car shakes as they go over bumps.

That evening as she lies in bed, propped up with pillows and staring at the wall, Anna considers her situation. Anatomically, she has never been so healthy or so unhealthy, especially at the same time. She would like to call someone, but she has been too busy exploring the limits of her possibilities to have friends. She hasn't even made a place in her life for a cat.

Depressed, she reaches for her drawing pad and braces it against her bent knees with her left forearm, an effort that costs her something. Within a few minutes she creates Pain Gain, a board game where you advance by placing yourself or your competitors in difficult situations; Shield, an air freshener and reality screening device that "limits your perceptions so you don't have to"; and Mystique, an underarm deodorant and charisma enhancer "that gets you places you've never been before."

Bored, she thumbs through *Swimming*, *Triathlete*, and *Runner's World* contemplating new equipment: a tankini racing suit, a cyclometer, one-hundred-fifty-dollar running shoes. She thinks about doing another triathlon though the pain in her shoulder makes her feel sick when she imagines training, but thinking about quitting makes her feel worse. Maybe the physical therapists at the hospital can help her. Maybe she can use the whirlpool and train on the stationary bicycle. Maybe she will catch up with the others eventually and enjoy the benefits of her labors, but she is doubtful. Sinking back against the pillows, Anna sees her worlds overlapping, feeding each other dangerously like a meshing chain and sprocket turning faster on themselves. Perhaps she should reevaluate her goals.

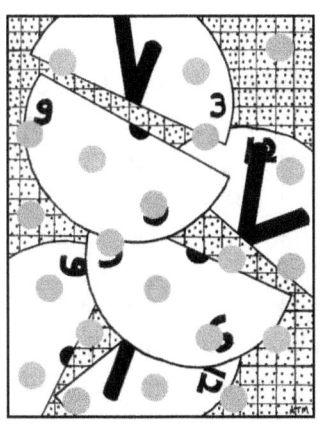

Say It Ain't So

MY STUDENT KIM—A COMPUL-
sive storyteller who's often absent,
tardy, or in some way impeded
from completing her creative writing assignments—sits in my
office in her wheelchair, strapped in because she has spasms
that cause her to rear back so her feet have to be tied down and
her lap loosely belted. She can't talk while this happens, and
her whole body strains with the effort—hands waving in the air,
fingers curled into claws. Otherwise she's cute—small and cur-
vaceous with curly blonde hair and a chirpy smile. Light scatters
across her blue eyes making her intentions opaque.

Kim—who's been absent for a week—explains she had
blood tests done and x-rays taken. She couldn't get a formal
excuse because the doctor couldn't find anything wrong, but
she hopes I'll excuse her anyway. I do. The students are the
customers—the president of this rural Pennsylvania state
college insists—which makes me the check-out clerk.

To look over her homework, Kim asks me to open the
backpack strapped to the back of her wheelchair and remove
her black binder—there are several of them, color-coded by
subject. I sit down facing her, open it, and turn to the fiction
exercise I asked her to rewrite because the original was
incoherent, a scene where she talks to her mother about her
mother's boyfriend. She uses her own name, and it appears to
be nonfiction, except there's no information about her being in
a wheelchair. Only one of my students has written about having

77

a significant physical impairment though ten percent of my students do.

The assignment was to have one character in denial about something talking to another character who knows the truth. As I read, I realize Kim's first draft wasn't sloppy. Information was selectively edited out. What was missing in the first version and included in the second is that her mother's boyfriend is bisexual, and it's her mother's boyfriend, not her natural father, whom she calls "Dad."

"Why isn't Dad sleeping over tonight?" she asks her mother in both renditions of the scene. "You know you love him."

The reason Dad isn't sleeping over is because he's with a guy, Kim writes this time.

"This makes more sense," I respond.

Kim laughs awkwardly, lurching back with one of her seizures, then tells me why she was sick. On the phone her mother asked if she had plans for summer vacation. She said no. Her mother said she'd better make some because she wasn't allowing her to come home. Kim laughs some more, and I expect the happy ending to be that her mother has changed her mind, but it isn't.

"She meant it?" I ask. "You really aren't going home for the summer?" Telling your child with serious disabilities she can't come home isn't something you can share with your friends and get support for, I don't imagine.

Kim laughs again, pulling back a snort through her nose, then says, "It's all true. The truth makes the best stories."

Kim explains that her personal care attendant, Diane, who is like a mother to her and has two teenaged boys herself, was out sick for a week, which caused the crisis between Kim and her mother. Kim's mother is jealous of how close Kim is to Diane. Kim's mother isn't able to make close friends like Kim does. She doesn't listen to people. Her mother has been best friends with her boyfriend for twenty years and still won't tell him that she loves him, Kim says.

But what is really upsetting her, Kim finally divulges, is that she is afraid she and Diane aren't close any more. They are having difficulties because the rumor around the handicapped students' dorm is that Kim is having an affair with Diane.

Kim reminds me—she has told me this before—rumors about her being gay were spread last year in her dorm because people were jealous of how close she was with another female student with disabilities, her best friend. On the first day of class when I asked students to talk about how they had influenced others through the power of the word, Kim shared how she had convinced this friend not to commit suicide. Afterward, Kim told me she hoped her ability to affect people with her words wouldn't frighten me. It wouldn't, I said at the time, but already she has led me beyond my bearings into a landscape she controls.

Kim says that since the beginning of the semester she and Diane haven't been able to talk because if it looks like they are too close they will be in trouble, but when Diane returned from being sick, Kim broke down and told her everything. Kim has been so upset that she is back on antidepressants, and those—or something—this is why they did the blood work and the x-rays—are making her sick. She was absent because she could not stop throwing up.

I ask Kim to stop talking so I can make corrections on her next piece where she tells this in writing. She laughs as I question her and put her responses down.

"It's all true," she repeats. She arches back in her chair, her smile stretched into a grimace. When her body relaxes, she completes her thought. She has so many stories to tell.

My phone rings. A female colleague across the hall asks if I need help.

"No, I'm fine," I say and thank her, wondering why she called. Maybe I was talking too loud. I've gotten in trouble for that before.

I turn back to Kim who explains that Diane can't be her personal care aide in the summer. Diane has to have time off to keep her sanity and be with her boys. But Diane is helping her find an apartment and a personal care aide and apply for jobs. Diane is willing to be a job reference, Kim boasts, as though Diane's word is all that will be required for her to find work.

Kim has been to visit Diane at home many times. Diane likes the understanding she gives her, Kim says, and she is careful not to make Diane's boys jealous of her friendship with their mother. "The boys like me," she states proudly, "and I want it to stay that way." She has to learn to trust herself. She hasn't overburdened Diane. She knows they are still close. Her mother accuses her of clinging to people, but she knows she is not clinging to Diane. She has to listen to her heart.

I nod and think *No clinging*, a requirement I have often failed to pass, and I am not physically dependent on others for my survival.

There is one last thing I must do—go through the syllabus to check Kim's late homework. Three of the missing assignments are in the black binder, she says, but they are handwritten. I require typed work and she wants to fulfill the requirements, but she types very slowly, she informs me, her arms waving in the air, her knuckles permanently humped. She dictates her writing to the study aide who writes it down, but according to someone's rules—the school's or the government's—she doesn't know whose—study aides are not allowed to type for those they assist.

I have not heard this from my other physically impaired students, but I agree it seems unfair, especially since all Kim needs a study aide for is typing. She is being trained on a voice-recognition computer, but her training is not complete. It is difficult for her to get someone to type her homework, which is why it is always late. I tell her maybe I can let the typing part go. I sometimes do this for other students, I assure her. I don't say it is my able-bodied students who often don't have access to computers. My special needs students always have whatever they require.

When our conference concludes, I stand and help Kim back out the narrow doorway. My office is too small for her to turn around. She can't see where she is going, but with my directions, she adjusts and readjusts the power control knob on the arm of her wheelchair until she is in the hall. She promises if she doesn't get hit by a truck and nothing more goes wrong, I will see her in class.

And I do. A few minutes later there she is, her back to the front of the classroom because it was easier for her to stop than turn around. Also, by facing the other students it is easier for them to help her, which they regularly do. Seeing the students' kindness to each other is one thing I like about my job.

The next class Kim doesn't show up; instead, one of her friends—a smaller frailer young blonde in a wheelchair—rolls in about fifteen minutes late. She is here to take Kim's place. She is here to listen for Kim so Kim can get the homework assignments straight. This substitute student likes creative writing and has sat in class with Kim before. I wonder how she fits it into her schedule, but she and Kim seem to operate inside a different understanding of time than I do, coming and going as they please.

"Get to class," I say to Kim when she calls a few days later to ask if it will be all right if she turns her homework in late. One more lesson on the voice-activated computer and she will be able to get her work done, her trainer has told her.

At the end of the next class, after the other students are gone, Kim tells me in a hushed voice because it is important no one hears, she missed class because just as she was going, Diane called and said there was an emergency meeting Kim had to attend. They were threatening to fire Diane. The rule that personal aides and those they care for are not supposed to develop close relationships is more serious than I'd imagined.

"I'm sorry I had to miss class," Kim says in spasms that are between pleading and apologizing. "Diane was going to lose her job. I had to be there for her."

"It's okay. You did the right thing."

"Everything is such a mess. I don't know what I'm going to do." She laughs, but it is only a leftover part of a pattern now.

"You'll make it. You're tough." She must be if she has gotten this far.

Kim has to appear before the board again and might be absent another day.

"It's okay. It's okay. You're doing the right thing."

As we leave the room Kim promises I will read all about "you know who"— she is afraid to say Diane's name out loud—in the poem that is due. The assignment is to write about a person, animal, or thing. I nod and smile understandingly then hurry off, overwhelmed by the machinery she is at the mercy of.

Telling stories may be the greatest power Kim has, but it is not enough. She is absent another week. I call the Office of Students with Disabilities and talk to the director. He tells me she's having problems in all her classes and always has.

"She's not really mature enough to handle college. Not everyone is."

When I finally get her poems, left in my mailbox, handwritten on lined paper, they are about the problems we have been discussing—who is a true friend, whom can you trust, whom can you love—but they are dated from when Kim was in high school. I could plug Diane's name into every one of them, but Kim didn't know Diane then.

The next time I see Kim, she is in the office of the chair of the English department getting a complete withdrawal from all her courses. A few minutes later, she wheels across the English department parking lot. She is going home.

In the People's Art Museum

I BECOME MORE INCOHERENT AS each day I am less understood. I say so little I have nothing left to say. Words flutter from my life like trapped birds frantic to escape, a blur of good intentions poised in flight, Cassandra scrawls in her notebook. She stops, afraid she's headed nowhere, where the Mad Inquisitor always says she heads, and looks around her favorite retreat, her suffering northeastern city's stone amphitheater, fragmented and forgotten.

Earlier in the afternoon as she was leaving the Mad Inquisitor's party, where *he* had such a good time, he had asked her, hopefully, "Are you going to put *this* into a story?" meaning the event he had created and the lovely way he saw it.

She had smiled and said, "No, probably not. There are too many stories like it." That finally crushed him.

After their last evening together, when she tried to kiss him and he wasn't interested, she didn't want to see him again. But she had to go to his party, he said. He was getting together all the best people, a whole collection of interesting types.

She picks up her pen to begin again.

On a post-industrial downtown sidewalk a tall gawky man wearing a tuxedo and top hat and carrying a cane (the Mad Inquisitor to be exact) *observes a hat—a bowler—under a ladder. Fearing for his life, he breaks the sacred triangle—*

Father, Son, and Holy Ghost—and walks under the ladder, hat held before him.

He carries it inside the brownstone building it was lying in front of, up the flight of stairs, curious to find the owner. He finds a door, knocks, and is welcomed in, hat first, to the People's Art Museum. Here all the people are art. They stand in frozen classical positions, webs of pink fiberglass.

"Every quarter hour they change positions," the Hostess in a white Grecian robe explains. "On the hour, tea and cookies are served to all, and you may interact with the art."

She takes the bowler and places it on the head of a nineteenth-century man. "Thank you," she says. "He must have set it on the window ledge, and it blew off."

The Mad Inquisitor nods.

The Hostess takes his top hat and cane and has him sign the register. All the great people who have ever lived have been here, he notices right away, and penning his name, assumes his rightful place in history by being a patron of the People's Art Museum. It's just as he has been telling the young woman, Ms. Deliberate, all along. One must get out and do things, one must take one's place in the celebration that is life. Ms. Deliberate, with her long face and condescending introspective ways, will get nowhere. She'll never be allowed inside the People's Art Museum. He puts down the pen and straightens himself smugly.

The Mad Inquisitor introduces himself to the Defining Cook and the Harpy Teacher, two of the most agreeable statues in the twentieth-century room. If only Ms. Deliberate were here, he thinks, *she could see how real women behave. Whenever someone tedious approaches, the Harpy Teacher bares her hidden beak tooth and thin-skinned pink mouth with a raspy throaty hiss. Pink talons appear from the sleeves of her shiny blue-green dress. She covers her whiteboard with confetti-colored responses as questions punctuate the air.*

At every turn in the conversation, the Defining Cook assists. She reads from a diet book held by her pink hands in front of her round face, the rest of her wrapped tightly in a white apron like a package of meat.

"Water," she says. "For good health it is necessary to have eight full glasses of water a day. Carrots. Carrots are one of the most affordable sources of vitamin A."

Meanwhile, Ms. Deliberate sits at her desk, glad to be away from the Mad Inquisitor, at least temporarily. As she searches for something to write about, a neighbor boy appears outside her window. She puts him into a story. He's floating, face down, in an enormous indoor swimming pool. It's early morning and barely light inside the vaulted structure. He floats easily, lungs stopped full of air, fingers waving gently through the water like two persistent schools of tiny white fish. Beneath him he sees a drifting forest of giant seaweed decorated with other bright darting fish—gold, black, lavender, fluorescent green. He flexes his body for a surface dive and swims for a conch attached to a nest of kelp twenty feet down.

Surfacing with the silvery pink shell, he spies the Niña, the Pinta, and the Santa Maria sailing into the New World. They arch over the brief horizon of the chlorinated sea so close they nearly suck him under. He waves the conch toward their dark bows. His greeting is returned with happy shouts from sailors anchored to the decks by the flared legs of their white pants. Pulling the meat from the conch with his hand, he blows to them in a vibrating moan, the first sound they have heard from an inhabitant of the future. The sailors continue waving as the three ships slide on. The boy is only five and has not yet learned to read. The names of the ships escape him.

Ms. Deliberate is interrupted by a knock at the door. She opens it. The Mad Inquisitor has come to visit, full of his adventures.

"You should meet the Harpy Teacher," he begins, stepping in and removing his top hat without being asked. "Just met her myself. Wonderful woman. From England originally, I believe. Speaks the King's English properly anyway. Not some Philistine. You should meet the Defining Cook though you probably wouldn't get along. Not important really. I often get along by not getting along at all. What's important is that she studied in France. All the best cooks do, you know. Never been there myself. Often thought of going. Have you tried that marvelous French restaurant? Can't think of the name, but you know the way there, don't you?"

"What way?" she asks, hanging his things on the rack beside the door.

"What way to France? Well, flying is the best way. What way to England? Nice to take a boat. Nice if you have time. Nice if you can afford it. You should get out. Do something nice for yourself. Doesn't matter what. Try that restaurant I spoke of."

"What restaurant? I'm not hungry. I'm busy. I'm writing."

"Busy? Writing? You're always too busy, too busy for life. Why, I wrote myself this morning. I wasn't too busy. I wrote myself a little note. It was brilliant, I believe. Can't remember it now. Good thing I wrote it down. Important to be able to balance things: life and art, business and pleasure, reality and dreams. This is precisely where you fall short. Never a dream. Never a positive thought in your head. Always writing, writing, writing. I suppose if I were to say I had a black cat, you would say that you had one that was blacker. That is just where your sort of thinking leads."

"Where did you meet these people?" she asks, making tea. It's the only remedy for this sort of thing; then, she realizes it's not a remedy, it's only a habit. The remedy would be to hand the Mad Inquisitor back his top hat and cane and show him a generous opening of the door, but that's only another sort of habit. She dislikes how her thinking deteriorates around him just in proportion to the amount of spontaneity he encourages.

"Met them at the museum. Lovely cultural experience. You ought to go sometime. Nothing much happening here."

She sets the tea things on the low table in the living room, lights incense, and puts her prayer beads back in their cedar box. She turns on her music from outer space, hoping to calm the Mad Inquisitor. They sit on cushions, and she tells him her story.

"I think the fish represent hope. They often do."

"Hope? Not much hope here. If you really wanted to be inspired, you'd come with me to the People's Art Museum."

"But I have a lot to do. I've left the boy floating in the water."

"The boy can wait. This museum is a really special thing. Seems to have been around forever but might not last too much longer. Never say no to an adventure. Nothing ventured, nothing gained. Cats got your tongue? Rats make you run? Pick any topic. Someone's bound to be fluent on it. Come on, finish up that spot of tea."

She puts on an Indian striped madras skirt, a Javanese batik top, a Navajo turquoise necklace, and Mexican huaraches. The Mad Inquisitor fails to notice the appropriateness of her outfit for the People's Art Museum.

They head out of her neighborhood. The red brick buildings are crumbling. Dry weeds and garbage are everywhere. She strains to see any sign of life. Occasionally, she spots a dog or a cat in a window, but when she gets closer she usually discovers they are ceramic or cloth.

She complains, "It isn't right, the way people have to live here."

"Wrong, right—who's to judge?" the Mad Inquisitor says, twirling his cane. "Make no assumptions. That's my rule. You'll never be disappointed."

"That's a little pessimistic, isn't it?"

"No, of course not. Can't think of a better philosophy to live by."

She continues to peer into the buildings, falling behind. She hears a splash. Behind the iron bars of a row of basement windows she discovers the boy from her story swimming in a beautifully tiled natatorium. Gold and green seaweed and fish are glazed on the walls. He looks up and waves. She waves back. She calls to the Mad Inquisitor, but he's too far ahead to hear. Other children float in the blue water. She's sure she will not be believed if she explains what she saw, so she moves on.

When they reach the museum, a maroon feather boa is draped on the ladder under the window.

"Obviously, they're expecting us," the Mad Inquisitor says. "The red carpet's out and everything."

He flings the boa over his shoulder, climbs the ladder to the museum, and slips through the open window. She follows him.

The twenty-first-century gallery is closed for deconstruction, the sign says, so she trails him into the twentieth-century gallery. It is filled to capacity. The figures can barely move. This represents overpopulation, she assumes. Assume nothing, she reminds herself, but she can see that across the way in the nineteenth-century gallery there is more space. She is pushed this way and that, her bare arms stinging from the pink fiberglass art.

She wonders what to do about the boy and the other children she has left without a lifeguard. Is someone looking for them? Is she responsible for them? She can't go around creating characters and abandoning them recklessly. It defeats the purpose of starting at all.

Finally, she sees the Mad Inquisitor coming toward her, parting the pink gauzy crowd with his cane and his elbows. She recognizes the Harpy Teacher who accompanies him.

When they reach her, the Harpy Teacher bares her talons and hisses.

"Oh no," he says. "This is the young woman I've been telling you about, the one I wanted you to meet."

The Harpy Teacher pauses in mid-hiss, her beak tooth bared and a rasping cry stuck in her throat. She looks toward the Mad Inquisitor. He nods, and she extends her curled talons toward Ms. Deliberate in a gesture of hesitant greeting, the cawing sound dissipating from her lips in short bursts.

Two statues—men in dark blue business suits—one with a cowboy hat and boots, one with a top coat and fedora—walk up to them, connected by a telephone cord secured around their wrists.

The man with the cowboy hat tips it toward Ms. Deliberate and smiles. "Make any money at it?" he says in greeting.

The man in the fedora touches his hat and asks with enthusiasm, "What's the bottom line?"

They introduce themselves as the West Coast Man and the East Coast Man. The Harpy Teacher, still trying to get at Ms. Deliberate, becomes entangled in the cord, and the three statues wrap around each other.

"There's the Ingenue!" the Mad Inquisitor shouts, taking Ms. Deliberate's hand and dragging her toward a statue of a beautiful young woman, about nineteen, with dark wavy hair parted on the side in a classical cut, a salmon-colored wool sweater, and a matching salmon-and-black plaid skirt. Her face curves up toward the corner of the room to expose her long neck and the fine straight line of her nose.

"Isn't she perfect!" he says, walking around the Ingenue. "Bright, too. Talked to her earlier. Knows her ABCs forward and backward in English and French. Quite an accomplishment for a college student these days. Shows initiative. An interest in life. Might take some tips from this one."

"Parlez-vous français?" Ms. Deliberate says, hoping to impress him, but he is inspecting the rich texture of the Ingenue's wool skirt.

There aren't many visitors at the museum, so the statues they have met gather around them, proud to be seen talking to guests. The Ingenue is the Harpy Teacher's protégé, Ms. Deliberate gathers from the way they support each other.

"Communication lines are growing," the Mad Inquisitor comments.

"Faulty prepositions are still a problem," the Harpy Teacher says.

"Faulty propositions are an even larger one," the Ingenue adds.

"Faulty preparation can spoil the soup," the Cook contributes.

The East Coast Man and the West Coast Man say in unison, "You've got your bottom line and your top line. You've got your red line and your black line. You've got your assembly line and your fault line."

Ms. Deliberate wants to say something, to join in, but the Mad Inquisitor bends toward the group in such a way that they all move forward, and she is left out. Still anxious *to prove herself, she reaches for the nearest museum pieces, the Ingenue and the Cook, and fixing her hands upon their shoulders, pushes them apart.*

The Harpy Teacher hisses.

"Don't you know the rules!" the Ingenue shouts. "Everyone else was playing very politely!"

An alarm sounds. The Hostess rushes over with an armed guard.

"You mustn't touch the art!" the Hostess says.

Ms. Deliberate grips tighter and pushes more, trying to include herself by jostling the whole group. They are all shouting and complaining now. The guard grabs one of her arms and the Hostess grabs the other. Her hands come away with fluffy chunks of art. As the sculptures push and pull at each other, the air fills with pink webs. Ms. Deliberate looks at the Mad Inquisitor in horror as she is dragged away. Perhaps now he will understand why she doesn't like to leave her apartment.

As she is escorted out, she sees the gold and white guest book on its stand in the marble foyer. She longs to have written her name in it. Instead, she finds herself stumbling along the cracked sidewalk, crying, worried about the damage she has done to the art, and wondering what to do with the pink fiberglass she holds in her hands. She's sorry she couldn't get along with the museum pieces the way the Mad Inquisitor does. She's sorry she cannot be this thing and that, that she cannot make herself up every day. She, too, is bored by her own constrictions.

Finally, she stops crying, knowing it does no good, deposits the prickly art remains in the trash, and heads toward her favorite hideaway, an abandoned outdoor theater with fractured stone seats. She hopes the sculptures can be patted and smoothed back into shape and that the attention they receive will be worth the trouble she has caused them. She hopes the Mad Inquisitor will talk about her in a way that amuses him and the others. She decides to send the boy and his friends in the pool home to warm suppers. One by one she removes the splinters of glass until she feels comfortable in her own skin again.

Cassandra puts her pen down. Across the rubble-covered field, she sees Ms. Deliberate coming toward her and goes to meet her. They huddle together, heads bowed down, arms clasped around each other as the wind comes up, and it grows cold and dim. *Will they put us in the People's Art Museum?* Cassandra wonders. *Probably not*, she decides. *In this broken neighborhood of shadow people, we will be their statue, their cultural memorial of hope,* she thinks, though the dark-clothed masses going by do not seem to appreciate their pose either. *We are as foreign here as anywhere else,* she concludes.

It is time to go home. The wind beats their long skirts as they watch their peasant sandals move over rocks and shattered bricks. They know the way, so they don't look up often. They walk for a long time; then, from the streets the Mad Inquisitor joins them. Wrapping his arms around them, he insinuates himself between them. The wind whips aside his chatter, and they are glad they can no longer hear him.

Boundary Lines

MY NEXT-DOOR NEIGHBOR, Alice, a flashy full-figured Teutonic-type, is the high school guidance counselor in this northern Allegheny foothill town. When she's not at work, she's entitled to do whatever she pleases, my neighbor across the street, June, a retired grade school teacher, explained to me. Alice devotes herself to her front yard, but on the side where my windows face, her devotion ends. Six-foot-high weeds flourish. Trash and leaves overflow a recycling bin posed on a stump. A shiny metal garbage can holds the birdseed she feeds the birds that come to my quince tree.

A year ago when I took a college teaching job and moved here, hoping to settle down, I told Alice how nice her front yard looked then asked if she could move her garbage can and recycling bin. She shook her head no. I hid the garbage can behind my quince. She moved it back. I felt ashamed.

Alice is proud of her new house, a gray prefab the size of a doublewide trailer. She's divorced and raised her children alone, so she probably saved for it her entire life. Before that, June said, Alice rented different houses in the neighborhood. She must have known this was where she belonged. I've lived all over the country, mostly in small towns like this, like the town I grew up in, but I left home because I didn't belong. All day I think of places I would rather be.

Alice adorns her front yard for each season. In the fall, she brought home cornstalks from a farm nearby and giant plastic pumpkins with lights inside from Walmart and created an arrangement near my house featuring a witch. For Christmas, she draped chains of plastic poinsettias and little lights over everything. At Easter, she found colored plastic eggs more than a foot long and almost a foot high and covered her lawn as if it were an Easter basket. All year, through wind and rain and snow and dark of night, a large American flag flies from her porch.

Near the street, along the side of my lawn, Alice's rock garden grows. A small American flag drags sideways into the dirt from a plastic support. Low pastel-colored flowers flow over the rock border. Tall bright-colored ones rise from the rocky center. People stop to admire it and talk to her. When she weeds it, she leaves the dead weeds piled on my grass. The only thing I can figure is she forgets to pick them up.

"At least she weeds your side," June told me. "She could just let it go."

Warm evenings Alice sits on her porch swing watching her young son with Down syndrome ride bikes or shoot hoops with the neighborhood kids. On weekends she takes the whole gang to the lake or the mall. For family picnics Craig's old babysitters are included. I think Craig must be the result of a mid-life affair. I think Alice's two grown children have a different father.

"I finally got my master's and got this good job," she once said, "then I got Craig."

In the center of her front yard tied to a stake is her aged basset hound with a long deep bark like a tape recorder played too slow. The sound of him trailing his chain down her front steps at six o'clock wakes me. Alice doesn't walk him because his arthritis is so bad he can barely move. I've never seen her clean up after him.

For Memorial Day weekend, Alice asks June to care for him so she can go away—drag him out of the house in the morning and drag him back in at the end of the day. June tells me she's scared the dog will die on her. His belly is covered with sores from lying on the ground, and his toenails curl back under his feet that are covered with a strange red fungus.

I use the time to clean out stuff the previous owner left in my garage, laying it on my lawn with a "free" sign. When Alice gets back she takes the two wooden ladders. One she throws in her backyard by the blue plastic kid's pool. The weeds haven't buried it yet, but they will. The other she paints dark green and sets near the birdseed can. She arranges a plant on each step and a Pittsburgh Steelers flag as the *pièce de résistance* sticking out of the top pot.

"How do you like my plant stand?" she asks her friend as I trim shrubs nearby. "I stole it out of her trash." Alice points at me like an alien trespassing.

Her friend approves of her ingenuity.

On a Friday night at the last high school dance of the year a teacher is shot and killed by a former student just returned from Afghanistan. Saturday morning, while news crews are in town, Alice is in her yard with her coffee cup inspecting her flowers. She had to know the teacher. The reports say he was active in everything—his church, the Boy Scouts, the volunteer fire and rescue squad. He had organized the dance where he was slain. Alice had to have been the kid's guidance counselor. According to the accounts, his fellow soldiers called him "Danny Death." He told his parents he thought he should assassinate some people. They were trying to get him help.

Sunday afternoon Alice's grown kids and their spouses and children gather for a barbecue. The men put up a swing set and cook hamburgers. The women bring loads of food from the house. There is a little table for the kids and a big one for the adults. When I was growing up, my parents had parties like that. They still do, with my brother, his children, and the neighborhood kids, but I haven't been home in years.

Monday and Tuesday, Alice stays late at work, consoling the bereaved, I presume. Wednesday, the day of the funeral, while I'm home having lunch, cars arrive. People get out with cakes and covered dishes. Alice's yard fills up.

Late that afternoon Craig's social worker stops by to shoot basketballs like he always does. Craig appears wearing a pair of women's black patent leather tap shoes and a pink Mylar top, its colors shifting in the light. He uses crutches to keep from sliding on the concrete in his tap shoes.

I'm on my remaining ladder trimming the tree in front with a hand saw. It isn't making noise like a power saw would, but as it falls dark, Alice walks my way. She reaches the ladder and puts her hand on it.

"You stop now," she says, pointing at me. "You've done enough."

I smile and keep sawing. *She is not my mother,* I tell myself, *and I am not her child.*

"That's enough! I've been watching you all evening. You stop and get in the house now. You don't need to cut that poor tree anymore."

Rather than argue, I get down.

The next evening when Alice comes home, I'm digging out a little bush that had some branches broken by the snow.

"You're not going to throw that away, are you?" she asks.

"Yes. It's all beaten up."

"If you're going to throw it away, I'm going to take it."

"No, you're not," I say, catching on quick, "because then I'd have to look at it growing in *your* yard."

"That's right." She smiles.

After she leaves, I stick the plant in a garbage sack and hide it in the trash can in my garage so she can't get at it.

June doesn't understand why two people as nice as Alice and I are can't get along.

Danny has been in jail since the night of the shooting. The military hasn't taken any interest in him, and his parents didn't ask for him to be out on bail. I picture him alone, hunched over on a cot, cornered and caged. He enlisted trying to improve his future—what we all try to do.

The day after Danny's arraignment, a man with a chainsaw comes to trim the ratty-looking jack pines on my property. He starts by cutting down a tree growing into my house, blocking the windows and causing the paint to mold.

June walks over shaking her head. She doesn't believe in taking out trees.

He trims the one near Alice's rock garden last. While he is roped up in the tree, chainsaw roaring, Alice strides out of her house and into my yard.

"I don't want you to do any more cutting until I get the surveyor to check these property lines." She points to the chainsaw man. "I don't want any more of these trees cut!"

Our exact boundary is unclear. Around here, people don't have fences. The yards just roll together, usually with shrubs between the houses for buffers. But this tree is at least ten feet inside my yard. I even told the guy not to trim the branches hanging over Alice's side.

"Okay," I say. "But it's my tree, and I want it trimmed."

Alice walks back inside. The guy finishes and hauls everything away. I measure from my house to find my property line. One edge of Alice's rock garden curves into my yard by six inches. I move the rocks and reposition the flowers, but there is nothing I can destroy or improve to get what I'm looking for.

The next week I notice Alice swaying on her porch swing every night while Craig plays by himself in the yard. She doesn't do any of her normal things, not even talk to her grown kids on her cell phone.

One evening while I'm weeding, she comes over.

"I'm sorry I got so upset about the trees," she says. "The noise was driving me crazy. I didn't want to see any more come down."

"That's okay. I didn't know it was such a big deal."

"My dog had just died. I'd had him since the kids were little."

I realize I haven't heard him bark or his chain rattle.

"I had to put him to sleep that morning. I just couldn't stand it."

I nod. A chainsaw is bad even on a good day.

"Why do the things you love have to grow old and die?" she asks.

They don't always grow old, I want to say. *Sometimes they die young.*

She shakes her head and starts to turn away.

"Mommy! Mommy!" Craig shouts, running to her, his arms spread wide.

She stands rooted to the ground as she strokes his head, his arms around her hips, his face pressed into her stomach in a way I can't imagine anyone having ever allowed me to do. I stare at them, lost in my own contentions. I don't even know what to want next.

Feng Shui

"I *AM NOT* YOUR GIRLFRIEND," Feng Shui calls out as she circles her bicycle around her boyfriend, Dog Boy, who's on his bicycle.

"Feng Shui" is not her real name; it's only the name she's been calling herself lately. "Dog Boy" isn't Dog Boy's real name either, but it fits him.

"You are too my girlfriend!" Dog Boy shouts.

"No, I'm not. You can't make me," she answers. She realizes this is true as she says it, finding it both satisfying and painful.

She speeds off through the oak-lined country lane slick with the wet gold leaves of fall. It's a Sunday afternoon, one of the few times both she and Dog Boy are free. Their lives are always sending them in opposite directions.

Glancing back she sees Dog Boy, who's never concerned about his lack of speed, following slowly. He wears a gray baseball cap and black sunglasses, a black scarf, gray and black sweatshirts, and black jeans. Feng Shui appreciates that even though he's poor, his outfits are carefully chosen.

They ride by the small dairy farm where she grew up. The house and barn are on one side of the road; the pasture with the cows lined up at the feed trough full of grain and migrating ducks is on the other. The road, and everything else, is covered with mud and cow manure. She waves at her younger sister, Eden, who passes by driving the tractor. Eden is perpetually smiling. She has long black braids and smooth brown skin like

Feng Shui does. They get their lush tropical coloring from their mother, a mail-order bride from the Philippines thirty years younger than their father. She left when Feng Shui was three. They've never heard from her.

Further down the road in the cornfields, Feng Shui spots something shiny and pink like a long balloon. When she gets closer, she sees it is a plastic blowup doll. She stops and gets off her bike, staring at it. The doll has no clothes on and no hole at the crotch where the leg seams meet. It's life-size but not very lifelike. Feng Shui supposes that's the point. She's afraid to pick it up though it's clean and apparently unused. The doll has a perfectly round mouth hole outlined in red, like lipstick, and lined with pink plastic. The lining is rather ungenerous, Feng Shui thinks, going only about two inches deep.

Dog Boy pulls up behind Feng Shui, gets off his bike, lays it gently down, walks over to the doll, picks it up, and stares it in the face. Dog Boy collects toys, usually G. I. Joe dolls, Matchbox cars, and Transformers, but he'll take anything. As a child, he hardly got toys. His father worked as a gravedigger here in eastern Pennsylvania, which is frozen half the year. Dog Boy helped him. There were rarely toys at Feng Shui's house either.

"You should take her home for your sexual partner," Feng Shui says.

"No, that's your job," Dog Boy replies, sticking out his chest and pointing at her.

Feng Shui laughs. The doll with its painted-on yellow curls and painted-on blue eyes looks like Dog Boy's Polish mother who was so beautiful as a young girl that Dog Boy cries whenever he looks at the one picture of her that exists from that time.

Dog Boy pulls off his belt, straps it around the waist of the doll, and straps the doll to his back using his back belt loop. He gets on his bike and heads to Feng Shui's.

"You look funny," she says as they pedal side by side.

"You do," he replies.

Feng Shui lives in the caretaker's house at the plant nursery where they work. Their boss, Mr. Halliburton, lives in a newly built mansion at the other end of the property. He and his family used to live in the house Feng Shui occupies. Business is booming. Dog Boy lives at home. His father is retired and takes care of Dog Boy's mother who has Alzheimer's. Dog Boy helps support his parents.

Dog Boy and Feng Shui met the year before when he was hired on the landscaping crew at the nursery. With his perplexed look and straight dishwater-colored hair hanging in his face, she thought he was cute, but he's a Libra. She's a Capricorn. To save pain and disillusionment, it's best they avoid each other, her astrology book says. The difficulties are too overwhelming. From the beginning, she sensed this was true, but she imagined him sweetly cuddling her, his light fingers playing her skin, their soft mouths inseparable. Soon she learned Dog Boy's fantasy was to tie her feet and hands together and spank her then have sex with only their genitals touching. When she comes home from dealing with customers all day, she doesn't feel the need to be spanked and tied up, so this is why he's bringing the doll to her house.

Arriving, they go into the living room. Dog Boy unstraps the doll and throws it on the soggy-looking brown recliner. Feng Shui puts her icy hands on Dog Boy's angular little face while Dog Boy pulls her hips toward his. She kisses him on the lips, a dry tight-mouthed kiss. She's given up French kissing him. His mouth is small and his tongue fills it leaving no room for her own. Besides, he doesn't like kissing. It's too personal.

"You're cold," he says.

"No, I'm not. I'm frigid." She laughs. To maintain harmony in their relationship, they pretend it's her fault they don't get very far when they try to be intimate.

Dog Boy shapes a mocking long "O" out of his mouth. "Ha, ha, ha. Very funny." He picks up the doll and aims his crotch at her open mouth.

"I can't wait until you get another girlfriend," Feng Shui tells him.

"Yeah, me too," he says, tossing the doll back in the chair.

Later, Feng Shui checks the three greenhouses as she does

every night and morning, making sure the temperature is steady and the misting system reaches all the plants. She begins at the greenhouse attached to her bedroom that holds the miniatures—roses with half-inch blossoms, bonsai trees that fit in the palm of her hand, shrubs the size of Brussels sprout buds. People come to the nursery from the surrounding towns and country estates, sometimes even from the cities hours away, looking for something to do, some unique way to kill time. The older ladies who buy these little plants talk to them in baby talk, cooing at them, tickling them.

Next she checks the seedling trees and shrubs then the flowering annuals, which are almost gone except for the chrysanthemums and some Christmas cactus. She used to believe in what she did. Now she doesn't. There's nothing natural, she has come to understand, about filling landfills with trash bags of lawn trimmings, raked leaves, or dead annuals. There's nothing beneficent about pulling weeds, running edging machines or leaf blowers, or applying pesticides, fungicides, herbicides, or chemical fertilizers. Controlling nature's chaos throws everything out of order.

Feng Shui ends her rounds at the shed that serves as an office for her and her coworker, Rip, who runs the landscaping side of the business. Rip is a former hippie with a long graying ponytail and a beat-up hippie van. He's supposed to be her mentor since he's worked here for years, but he's not supposed to be her boss. He is Dog Boy's boss. Feng Shui is supposed to be her own boss, taking care of the customers, the greenhouses, and the rows of trees and shrubs outside in the ground, but it doesn't exactly work that way.

She and Rip have made a little deal. He takes some plants, sells them on the side, and keeps the cash. He expects her to keep enough extra growing to cover it up. In return, he doesn't tell Mr. Halliburton to get rid of her. Every week Rip takes Feng Shui's inventory report, checks it, signs his name to the bottom, and presents it to Mr. Halliburton. It minimizes the contact between Feng Shui and the old man and makes Rip look good.

"Peace," Rip says when he takes the list from her. He bows

slightly, pressing his hands together in front of his heart. He's a practicing Buddhist, and dealing with him teaches Feng Shui to be very Zen. She must have no ego and no anger because Rip has more than enough of both.

"I thought we were going to be partners," he said the first time he took credit for something she did, and she told him what she thought. "If I'd known we weren't going to get along, I wouldn't have told Mr. Halliburton to hire you."

Rip had nothing to do today on his day off, it appears as Feng Shui walks into their office, and so moved the computer from the corner table where they could both use it onto his desk. A stranger coming in would assume Rip was in charge and she was his assistant, which is how it actually is. She assists in reflecting back to him the image of himself he wants to project whenever she thinks it's best not to fight with him, which is becoming all the time. On his desk where people's photographs of loved ones go, Rip has a picture of himself staring off into nothing and appearing completely self-contained.

Above his desk he hung a recent newspaper clipping of himself and the award they got from the Chamber of Commerce for helping to beautify downtown. They donated seeds for school children to grow in paper cups then supervised the planting of the flowers. It was Feng Shui's idea—she planned the colors and designs to promote prosperity for all and did most of the work. But when the photographer scheduled the picture, Rip went by himself. It wasn't until it was published that she knew about it. "Sorry it didn't work out to include you," he said.

Saturdays are the nursery's busiest days, and this Saturday is "Sweetest Day," one of those occasions commandeered by Hallmark that Feng Shui hates. At 5 a.m. she gets up. For luck she puts on the gold four-leaf-clover earrings Dog Boy gave her.

That afternoon as she advises one of their biggest customers, Mrs. Grabinski, where to place a plant to keep negative energy from entering her house, Feng Shui notices Mr. Halliburton walking in. He gives Feng Shui the evil eye. A line has formed at the cash register. Feng Shui excuses herself.

"It's always so nice to talk to you," Mrs. Grabinski says.

Feng Shui smiles and nods.

While she rings up customers, Feng Shui hears Mrs. Grabinski tell Mr. Halliburton, "Rip was at the house yesterday. I asked him what kind of shrubs you had in stock, but he didn't know a thing."

"He should." Mr. Halliburton gives Feng Shui an evil look again. "I get an itemized inventory list from him every week."

After Mrs. Grabinski leaves, Mr. Halliburton tells Feng Shui, "I want to speak to Rip when he gets back."

When the landscaping crew returns, Feng Shui tells Rip what Mrs. Grabinski said.

"I demand an apology from her!" Rip shouts.

"Just let it go," Feng Shui suggests.

When Rip returns from talking to Mr. Halliburton, he's smiling.

"This stuff needs to be loaded up," he says, handing Feng Shui an order to be delivered to Mrs. Grabinski Monday morning. "Sorry I can't help. I have to go to a sweat."

Feng Shui stares up at his imposing face with her mouth glued shut. Rip and his hippie friends often spend weekends sitting around in tepees purifying themselves.

Between customers, she loads the plants on the delivery truck. The landscaping crew, including Dog Boy, helps, but at four o'clock Mr. Halliburton tells them to go home. Feng Shui doesn't get off until five and has to finish up.

She's closing out the cash register when Dog Boy appears holding a small wrapped box. She can't take it because her hands are dirty.

"Where's my present?" he asks.

"What for?"

"Sweetest Day, of course."

"I didn't get you one," she says. "It didn't cross my mind."

"Then I'm taking mine back," he answers, and he does. He strokes the bow with the palm of his flattened hand. "You never get me anything."

"That's not true." She buys him practical things like socks and underwear and yard gloves when she sees them on sale.

"I think it's over between us," Dog Boy says.

"Okay," she replies. Her back and leg muscles quiver from exhaustion, and she can't find anything worth arguing about.

He sets the gift on the cash register. "Give it as a prize to the next lucky customer." He walks away then comes back. "Forget that. I'll give it to my mom." He consoles himself with it as he leaves.

Before she locks up, Feng Shui goes to wash her hands. When she's finished, she reaches to check her four-leaf-clover earrings. One is gone. Panic grabs her heart. She is sure this means the relationship *is* over. That's what Dog Boy will think if she tells him. She wants the earring back. She wants it to be in her ear the way it was that morning, but it is as hopeless as trying to restore Dog Boy to whom she thought he was before she got to know him.

At her house, she gets out her phone. Saturday is the one date she and Dog Boy always have. They go to the local pizza place and order the same thing and sit in the same place and listen to the same bunch of old guys in red-and-white striped vests play the same requests on their off-key instruments. Pizza is not something you can go out for alone.

"Feed me," she says when Dog Boy answers.

After dinner, as Dog Boy drives her home, the guilt begins. She should invite him in, and they should have sex. This would satisfy him for a week or two, and for her—what would it do for her?

Dog Boy stops his truck.

"Do you want to come in?" she asks.

He shakes his head. "I think we aren't going to be together much longer. I think you're going to find someone else."

She's been thinking of that. "I doubt it," she says.

After he drives off, she goes into the living room where the blowup doll is in the reclining chair. She wonders what her present was. She picks up the doll, sits down holding it to her chest, and cries. Without Dog Boy to play with, her life makes no sense. What's she doing here, working for these people and living in this place? She feels lost in the forest. All she can see are trees, trees, trees.

Her phone rings. Holding the doll, Feng Shui answers it. It's Dog Boy wanting to know if he should bring back the bicycle pump he borrowed.

Feng Shui clings tighter to the doll, squeezing it so hard she's afraid it will pop. Her own mouth is stretched into an open circle like the doll's, and like the doll, she can't talk. *I miss you*, she wants to say, but she's crying too hard.

"I'm sorry," he says. He, too, is crying.

"I didn't think it would hurt so much," she manages to get out.

"Do you want me to come over?" he asks.

"Yes," she says, but the whole time she's shaking her head no. She can see her face blur as if it were a distant mechanical thing, a metronome that will eventually wind down. Only the doll appears to be alive, cheerful and optimistic, ready for anything.

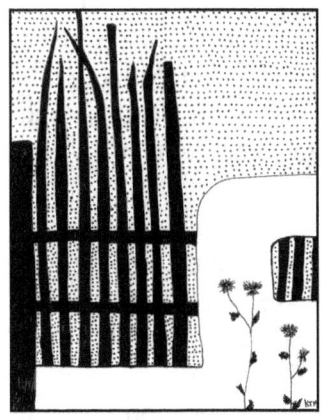

Intuition or Imagination?

"YOUR INTUITION IS GOOD. YOU can trust it," a psychic told me, which I thought was true, but my imagination skews toward the dramatic, so I struggle to keep the two separate and straight.

When I was offered a college teaching job in the northern Allegheny foothills, I asked her if I should take it. "You can stay there the rest of your life," she prophesied. I knew this was not good news.

My third winter, after one meeting in which my department head, a congenital liar, gave a particularly despotic performance, I left repeating, "I want to kill myself; I just want to kill myself" to a colleague. When she got home, she told her husband. He made her call the suicide hotline. They called me.

That summer, when therapy didn't help, I saw another psychic. Without speaking, I thought, *Should I leave Pennsylvania?*

"Yes. Definitely yes. You have to get out of there," she foretold.

I wondered, *Where should I go?* I had been imagining New York City or Taos, New Mexico, where I had once spent a month and knew someone.

"Taos. Definitely Taos," she divined.

Despite New Mexico having some of the highest rates of unemployment, poverty, alcoholism, domestic violence, and auto accidents in the country, I marketed my house, which I had bought for Uno, my aging rescued greyhound dog, and flew to Taos to find a place to live. The only thing I could afford was a three-room casita attached to the garage of a large house. As I looked across the landscaped garden to a huge pile of uncut logs I thought, *Someone has a chainsaw and heats with wood.* I bought the casita anyway.

I knew my new neighborhood of old adobe houses in the slum/historical district behind Taos plaza would be a terrible place to walk Uno. The streets were very narrow and the cars very fast. There were no sidewalks and barely any dirt edges. The high adobe and stick fences were built close to the asphalt. Dogs ran loose—big tough mongrels, combinations of wolf, Siberian Husky, Rottweiler, German Shepherd, Malamute, Chow. I was afraid Uno would get in fights with them.

When he was younger, he fought every dog that got near him and won every fight he had. I held his leash, screaming, as other people's loose dogs ran toward him.

"GET YOUR DOG!" I shouted to the owners.

"My dog doesn't fight!" they shouted back.

"MINE DOES!" I said.

Uno had his teeth in the other dogs as their owners told me, "Greyhounds don't bite. They're very gentle. I saw it on TV." Reality was not proof enough.

After the fall semester, I packed my new small SUV—the most expensive car I had ever owned—screaming at myself not to take Uno.

"You can't put him to sleep. You can't leave him behind," my neighbors said.

He quit eating dog food two days before we left. Migrating across America, I bought him fast food burgers and walked him every two hours. When some minor crisis, like passing through a city or hitting a traffic jam, forced me to slow down, he stood up, blocking my rear view. When I stopped at a light or changed lanes, I heard him thumping around as he struggled to balance on his reedy legs.

The afternoon of the third day, we traveled through Oklahoma on a four-lane road everyone treated like a superhighway. Cars tailgated each other at eighty miles an hour. At sunset—rush hour—I motored through Tulsa at seventy— dangerously below the prevailing speed—with Uno blocking my rear view and the sun in my eyes turning the freeway signs black. Ahead of me the highway divided and, nearly blind, I chose which fork to take. Since it was too risky to change lanes, I went for the nearest one. I was right, but later when I stopped at a service station, I was so shaken I left Uno, trembling with cold and fear, by the wall of the building. I didn't want to get killed over a nervous ailing dog; then, I went back for him.

It was late when we entered Oklahoma City's maze of intersecting freeways. After following branch after branch, trying to read unfamiliar signs in the dark, and because of Uno, having no view out the back when I changed lanes, we were finally on the outskirts of the city when I heard what sounded like a gunshot. It sounded like a bullet had hit my car. I looked around for someone shooting at me. The other drivers zipped along. The noise replayed in my head, and my ears rang. Something more powerful than my imagination was causing that. I saw a flash of blue and yellow light coming from the tailpipe of an old pickup that had passed by. I heard the sound again, but fainter. There it was, a truck letting off explosions in the night, and no one seemed to mind.

Later I saw the dent toward the back on the driver's side, just where I'd heard the noise.

A few days before Christmas, I wrapped presents for my family, anxiously watching the afternoon go by. Anything related to my family makes me anxious, and having to go to the post office inside Taos's biggest grocery store the last Saturday before the holiday made me panic.

The parking area was crowded with trucks and SUVs—large irregular vehicles driven out of the mountains—and beat-up economy cars from town. Shopping carts littered the lot. At the far end of the store, I pulled into a space with three abandoned carts next to it.

As I opened my door, a man and his daughter in a rusted pale blue truck appeared behind me. To avoid the carts, he was driving at an angle into my space. The only thing I could think was that he was going to take out the rear of my car. It probably wouldn't have dented his truck, and if it did, it probably wouldn't have mattered to him. I signaled to his daughter for him to stop. In a fear-inspired rage, I got out and dragged the carts away. The man looked at me with a slightly annoyed composure. He couldn't figure out what my problem was.

My instinct was to move my car, but I couldn't see a safer place to go. Standing in the post office line, I was so angry I couldn't talk. I wanted to leave, but I told myself that was silly. As I shopped for a few things I didn't need or couldn't find, I told myself my car could be being hit right now, but I refused to take myself seriously.

When I went out, my car was surrounded by more oddly formed vehicles. I had picked the junk car parking area. Ahead of me was an old pickup with an open camper top filled to the top with rubbish, including a ladder dangling out. How could the driver see to back in there and not hit anyone? I wondered.

Two days later I saw the dents on the front edge of my hood, as if someone had pressed two fingers into cookie dough ladder-width apart.

On the phone my independently wealthy friend, Ben, argued I was letting my imagination run away. Not every driver in Taos is drunk, he had to remind himself, or he would be in the same paranoid state I was in; then, because he didn't want to go out himself, he was sending his housecleaner to run errands for him and asked if I could pick up the bagels he had ordered for his party Christmas Eve. I reluctantly agreed.

At the bagel shop, I overheard some people saying someone had just rear-ended them on the highway then disappeared.

As I left the parking lot along the far side of the building, a barely running vintage pickup came toward me. The driver gave it extra gas as it sputtered and choked. When the hood popped up, blocking the windshield, he nursed the truck along, his head out the window. He passed me staring at the ground by his front tire. In my rearview mirror I saw the truck at a stop sign. The guy was still trying to get his engine going. He had not put down the hood.

Clinching the wheel with my thumbs on the horn, I drove outside of town to Ben's house. I didn't mention any of this as we set up for his party, afraid I would be ostracized for dealing in reality. Late that afternoon as I left his yard, I saw a small car angled off the road into the dirt and two guys observing it. The situation didn't look right, but I was headed in the other direction. I drove a short way, but because I thought I should be kind on Christmas Eve, I turned around.

By the time I got close, the car was resting across the middle of the asphalt. One of the guys lay face down in front of it. He wasn't hurt. He couldn't stand because he was so drunk. He kept raising up but didn't seem to know what to do after he got his stomach off the ground. His friend wandered by the car. Traffic was stopped behind them, but no one got out. The guy on the ground reached his hand toward me, white foam at the corner of his mouth. I didn't call the police. I knew they were not likely to come. I had called them twice when I found herds of horses—including mares with their colts—running loose as I ran at dawn on the narrow winding main road through the back of town. I had helped round them up.

At least those two guys would be asleep before the crowds for midnight mass were out tonight, I told myself as I turned around again. Hopefully, they wouldn't hit anyone before they passed out.

On New Year's Day, Uno and I were almost home from our earliest of five walks. I had them into a routine, timed to avoid the heaviest traffic. The cars went around us, or we stopped and waited for them. Four big dogs ran loose in our immediate area, plus others scattered along the way. Because he was so old, twelve, Uno was less aggressive than he used to be, but if they got near, he tried to attack. Most of the dogs were not vicious. They went away on their own, or if they didn't, I yelled

"GO HOME!" and kicked my boot toward them. They were more afraid of me than Uno.

The most aggressive dog we had come across was a poodle or Schnauzer mix, white and fluffy, with a plaid collar. The first time he chased Uno's hind end, barking and snapping, I thought he was much too small and frilly to be out alone. Something was going to happen to him.

New Year's morning I noticed four big mutts—two black ones, two tan ones with coyote faces—in the middle of a long curved dirt driveway, ganged up around what looked like a cardboard box or trash. I figured they had dragged it out of the garbage and were fighting over it. As I stared, I saw that the piece of trash was a little dog. I thought he was dead. His eyes bulged open, and he didn't move or make a sound. I thought he had been hit by a car in the night. I felt sorry for the owner. Maybe someone would carry him to the road and the owner would find him, or maybe the owner would never know what happened.

I walked on, telling myself not to go closer, not to be my usual morbid self, then had to go back. The little dog lay on the icy snow. I figured he was frozen stiff and rigor mortis had set in, but when one black dog picked him up and shook him, his legs flopped. He was still soft. As the dog put him on the ice, he adjusted himself then went back to playing dead. The attackers stood like overgrown bullies waiting for him to try to get away. I moved toward them. I didn't want them ganging up on Uno, but I had to do something to give the little dog a chance. As I got closer, one of the black dogs sank its teeth into him and dragged him away. The other dogs followed. They weren't going to let me take their prize.

I pulled Uno closer and moved toward the little dog. He played dead very convincingly, his eyes still open, not even his eyelids moving. I wondered if he could see his tormentors, or if he was in such a state of shock that he was blind. The coyote-faced dogs backed away, but the black ones didn't want to give him up. Not until I got right to the little one did they back off, lingering nearby, hoping to get their prey.

I knelt down and could see him breathing. He was soaked from the ice and snow, his skin the color and texture of a wet paper bag. Some of his hair had been ripped off in clumps. There were little hunks of furry meat on the ground and on him but not much blood. I was afraid he would bite if I touched him, but as I checked his tag he didn't move. He just played dead. I recognized his plaid collar.

It was maybe ten degrees, so I knew I didn't have much time. I didn't want to pick him up. I thought his back was hurt, or he could bite me and I would drop him. I needed to get help. I stood up and looked around. It wasn't far to my house, but I was afraid to leave the pack to finish him off.

I remembered seeing a young man come out of the house the driveway led to, the home of the two tan dogs, so I walked around the corner. A different young guy was inside eating breakfast, probably getting ready for work. It was before eight. I waved, but he didn't come out. I walked back to the little dog. He was still playing dead. I had to knock.

The guy didn't want to open the door, but I kept knocking and finally he answered. I explained what had happened. He put down his toast and rushed out. As he ran toward the injured dog, he asked if his dogs did the biting. "I don't think so," I said. He shouted that the black dogs lived behind where we were which was where they had finally retreated. They weren't dogs normally running loose.

By the time I got to the little dog, the young man said he knew whose it was. He ran across the street. I stayed with the dog as he lay on the ice, wet, with puncture holes in him. I knew being wet made the cold worse, but I didn't want to take off my coat or Uno's and get them wet and bloody, so I petted the little dog's head. I didn't know if I should even touch him. I knew he would never be the same. A friend once had a kitten stolen out of her house by a raccoon. The raccoon dropped it trying to get away. It wasn't hurt, but the trauma changed its personality.

After a few minutes, the young man came back. He said the dog's owner was coming. He went to get a blanket. He reappeared with a pale lavender comforter. I thought of the mess it would be after he wrapped it around the little dog, but he didn't seem to think of it. The owner of the dog, a young housewife, came with a blanket. I said I would get something to carry the dog in. I thought he shouldn't be lifted, that it would make his injuries worse. I ran off with Uno toward my house. I heard the dog bark sharply. I figured they had picked him up.

By the time I got back with a laundry basket, there was nothing in the driveway but the comforter and two small places marked with blood. I saw the young man's dogs at the door of a house across the street. I walked up to the door and knocked. The young man came out. I stared at the blood on his hands before he rushed off, probably late for work. I shouted "Thank you!"

I told the woman I was the one who found her dog. She was calling the vet. The phone at the other end kept ringing. No one was answering on New Year's Day. She told me her little girl had let the dog out to go the bathroom; then, she took her little girl to the bathroom; then, she called the dog, and he didn't come. It had only been a few minutes though now it had been a few minutes more. I thought of how cold he must be. He was probably just wrapped in a blanket without any heat and not generating much on his own. I gave the woman the basket and said I'd come back to see how he was. The phone was still ringing at the vet's.

All day I thought about the little dog, how horrible it must have been to be attacked, of how people all over the world get attacked by other people the same way, and how I would feel if Uno got away and got hurt. He'd never been out by himself his entire life. Uno and I walked by the dog owner's house a couple of times during the day, but I didn't knock. I told myself to wait.

The next day as Uno and I were walking, a man was getting into a truck in the dog owner's yard. I asked how the little dog was. He said she had to put him to sleep. The vet said it would take three operations, and even then he might never be the same. He might die from the surgery. Also, his blood was so cold. They would have had to warm it up somehow. The woman had cried all day and was only now a little better. She had had the dog for ten years. They had lived there for six years.

They always let him out. He stayed in the yard; then, he began roaming farther and farther. That morning he roamed in the wrong direction.

"Live and learn," the man said.

I thought he was referring to the little dog, but whatever the dog learned while he lay on the snow, the other dogs hovering around him, he learned too late. At least he was with his owner, and she knew what happened to him.

A week later I read in the local newspaper that a man at Taos Pueblo had gone out to feed his horses and found the body of a fifteen-year-old boy lying in an ice-encrusted creek. The boy's head had been beaten and his body dragged from a dirt road to the water. A school photo showed the boy with a sweet defiant face, cheeks still puffy with baby fat.

According to the news story, the night before, native dancers had gone from house to house celebrating Epiphany, the day the Magi arrived with gifts for the Christ child. The teenager, who was raised by his extended family since his mother died when he was young, had gone out late visiting friends with his cousins. On his way home someone followed him. He was little for his age and alone. It was a dark night. The crime involved gangs, investigators thought. The young men of the community were divided, incredibly enough, between the athletes and those interested in jewelry-making. Threats of violence had been circulating, including a rumor the boy would be attacked.

I never did decide if bringing Uno was the right thing to do. After five months I put him to sleep. A year later I sold my casita. My neighbor not only had five chainsaws and a wood splitter for his firewood but a weed whacker he mowed his garden lawn with and a table saw outside his garage next to where my computer was. But in spite of everything, Taos was the right place to be for a while.

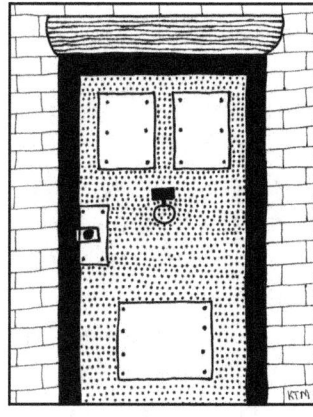

Saving Herself for Julian Markov

DRIVING TO THE SANTA FE airport, Tracy glances at the rearview mirror of her pickup. Her spiked short hair and boyish pixie face appear androgynous, indeterminate, which as an only child growing up on a New Mexico dude ranch kept her entertained, but now as an adult, people want her to stand for something, to put their fingers on her, to not be roaming around on the fringes of interpretation.

Tracy is picking up her friend from an artists' residency, Elaine, a freelance copy editor in New York. To save money, Elaine rents out her apartment and house-sits, which is why she is coming to Santa Fe. For convenience, she wears the people's clothes where she stays. She was wearing the plaid wool shirt of a famous young male writer when Tracy spoke to her last. Elaine's boyfriend's father, a famous editor, got her the job.

Elaine steps out of the airplane in a black sleeveless dress that shows off her slender white arms and angled cap of black hair with a sophistication Tracy finds unreal. Walking down the portable stairs and across the tarmac, Elaine appears translucent—distant and quixotic. In another life she could come back as cocaine.

"Tracy!" Elaine squeals, rushing to hug her then drawing back and looking her up and down.

As usual when she is around Elaine, Tracy feels like an oversized goon.

Tracy drives to her boss's house where Elaine is staying.

Gabriel—a commercially successful sculptor who does wall jewelry—enormous amorphous silver pieces embedded with semi-precious stones the size of rocks—is leaving on a spiritual retreat to India.

When they arrive at his pueblo-style adobe, Gabriel is fixing pumpkin seed mole for the blue corn enchiladas. His silver-streaked dark beard cascades down his pale blue work shirt. His dark hair curls around his shoulders. In his tight jeans he looks like a cross between a guru and a rock star. Tracy has a crush on him though she knows it is inappropriate. He is sick of women hating him, he told her as they kissed one night. He would rather be alone.

Throughout dinner, Gabriel stares at Elaine. He seems not to know Tracy is there. Shaking her head, Elaine sings insouciant lyrics by her surrealist musician friend: "She has to be true, true, true—one persona at a time." Tracy has never heard of him, but Gabriel has.

After dinner, to amuse Gabriel, Elaine tries on his leather hat, vest, and boots waiting by his suitcase. Gabriel stands transmuted, holding his work shirt toward her, his white arms sticking out of his T-shirt. Tracy is always impressed by Elaine's ability to play with people's minds.

Later, as Elaine sits between Tracy and Gabriel on the porch, she wears the black leather jacket she took from her boyfriend's apartment that morning. He will find it missing tonight. Gabriel wears an Indian blanket around his shoulders. Tracy wraps her arms around herself and leans her head back against the warm wall watching narrow gold clouds cross the cardinal-colored full moon that hangs too large and close. Nearby, coyotes howl.

After their bottle of red wine, Elaine, giddy, flirts with them both then pushes them away with her fingertips, throwing her head back, rolling her eyes. "You two are being positively lugubrious," she says, a word Tracy assumes is popular in New York. They ride like birds on the shifting drafts of Elaine's emotions.

As Gabriel sings Irish ballads with a voice that is round and deep, Elaine lays her sculptured adorable head against his shoulder. Tracy shuts her eyes. When Gabriel stops singing, Tracy opens her eyes to see him stoking the strands of Elaine's fine glossy hair.

Elaine stands and demands to be walked to bed. Tracy is reluctant to go, but Elaine holds out one luminous white arm, curved like a wing, and Tracy slides under it.

In the moonlight they settle Elaine on Gabriel's bed, and he lies next to her.

Tracy walks toward the door, but Elaine calls out, "Don't go, Tracy. Stay with me. Gabriel, don't you want Tracy to stay?"

Tracy turns and waits for Gabriel's answer. He looks silently at Elaine. Tracy turns away.

"Tracy, come on the bed with us," Elaine says.

Tracy stops to consider where she might fit in. She has never been to bed with a woman. Perhaps if they were lovers, she would trust Elaine more.

"Come on, Tracy," Gabriel says, reaching out his arm. Elaine smiles.

Tracy walks toward them, finds room to lie on her side on the lower part of the bed, and curls her head toward Elaine's stomach. Elaine pretends to sleep. Gabriel strokes Elaine's back while Tracy strokes Gabriel's thigh. She feels ridiculous when nothing comes her way.

When Gabriel leans over and kisses Elaine, Elaine turns and snuggles into him. Tracy withdraws her hand and waits what she hopes is a sufficient amount of time, gets up, goes into the guest bedroom, crawls into the bed, and lies rigidly in the dark. She is almost asleep when she hears the click of the light. Blinking, she looks at Gabriel and Elaine standing across the room.

"Tracy. What are you doing? Why did you leave?" Elaine asks.

"Are you all right?" Gabriel says.

"I'm fine. I'm trying to sleep. Go back to bed."

But they don't want to. Gabriel wants to sleep by himself. He goes to his room leaving Elaine behind. Tracy can't sleep in the same bed with her, so she wraps herself in the bedspread and lies on the floor. It does not make her feel any better that Gabriel and Elaine are sleeping apart.

In the morning, Tracy has to take Gabriel to the airport. Elaine refuses to go. "It's so terrible with the three of us together," she says as she kisses first Gabriel then Tracy goodbye, pecks on their cheeks. It is true, and stated by the person who least prides herself on being honest.

Tracy and Gabriel pull into the parking lot early. Gabriel leans against the front of the truck smoking a cigarette. Tracy bops around in her baggy jeans and cowboy boots, bumping her shoulder into him and making jokes. Gabriel tells her to calm down, but he's smiling at her.

Tracy notices a tall thin man in a cowboy hat get out of a faded yellow pickup. The man walks toward the terminal. Inside the truck a Native American boy, maybe eighteen years old, stares straight ahead at them.

When Tracy looks again, the boy has gotten out of the truck and is walking toward them with the rigid stare of an automaton. He is about her height and dressed as she is except he has two black braids hanging against his T-shirt. Tracy looks to see where he might be headed. He is headed at her.

She stops bouncing and moves closer to Gabriel who stares off over his cigarette. She smiles at the boy to break the malicious glow coming from his eyes. When he doesn't respond, she realizes he must be on drugs, maybe PCP, something that makes you capable of acting without thought.

She grabs the arm of Gabriel's shirt. He looks down at her with philosophical disinterest. She tries to hide behind him, but he steps aside, exposing her more. The boy's eyes are locked on her. He is only a few feet away. He does not slow down. His hand comes up, palm first, and shoots toward her chest as if it had a task on the other side of her body. When he hits her, his arm does not give. She staggers back, the wind partly knocked out of her.

The kid looks at her, seeing her a bit for the first time, and asks angrily, "Do you know what you *are*?"

She knows he is accusing her of being a guy, of being gay, of being what he is—a young boy with an older man—since she looks like him. She has been mistaken for a guy before.

"Sure, I know what I am," she says, leaving it for him to figure out.

The feminine sound of her voice confuses him. Going soft for a moment, he looks at her then Gabriel. Tracy pulls Gabriel's arm. They could run for the terminal. This could be over. It's the Santa Fe airport in the middle of the day for Christ's sake. There doesn't have to be an Indian battle scene.

Gabriel won't move. His manhood is on trial, Tracy supposes. The young Indian's eyes flash from Tracy to Gabriel and back. He understands they are not two guys together, but he still has all that rage that needs somewhere to go.

"Come on, Gabriel. Let's get out of here." Tracy tugs at him, thinking she has to protect him, that she can't leave him behind. But she realizes Gabriel is big, and she doesn't have to stay. She runs toward the terminal feeling nothing but sorry for the kid. She looks back to see them squaring off, holding their fists up at each other.

Inside the small terminal she shouts, "There's a fight! Call the police! There's a kid out there on drugs!"

Everyone lined up obediently at the ticket counter looks at her.

The tall cowboy walks toward her. "Where?" he says.

She points to the parking lot. Outside the man starts running. She follows him. Gabriel and the boy are still sparring. The man heads for his truck. When he gets to it, he stops, puts two fingers to his mouth, and blows as if whistling to a dog. The young Indian puts his arms down and looks around, leaving Gabriel without a target. The man points to the truck. Like a robot, the kid turns and walks toward it.

Tracy walks to Gabriel, watching as the kid gets in and sits staring ahead. The man gets in and closes the door. They drive off. The sun is shining amid puffy little clouds, and it's just another blue morning in the parking lot.

Gabriel and Tracy walk toward the terminal.

"Wow. That was scary. Are you okay?" Tracy asks.

"Yeah," he answers, not asking how she is.

Her chest hurts from being hit, and she's upset. She wants him to put his arm around her shoulder, but he doesn't.

"I think he thought we were gay," she says. She tries to hold his hand, but he won't let her. "I'm not a guy," she insists.

He looks at her skeptically.

In the terminal, she stands in line with him. As soon as he gets his ticket, he heads toward the boarding area. She waves and walks out.

At Gabriel's house she finds Elaine in the bathroom painting her fingernails pale shiny pink.

"I need girl lessons," Tracy says.

Elaine looks at her.

"Fix me up. Give me something to wear. Show me how to do make-up. I'll try anything." Tracy tells her what happened.

Elaine puts a wide pink ribbon around Tracy's short hair, paints her face, and sprays perfume on her. Tracy stands in front of the mirror dangling a silver feather earring from one ear and a plump pearl one from the other. Since she no longer recognizes herself, it's hard to judge.

"I know who'd be perfect for you," Elaine says.

Tracy raises her eyebrows.

"Julian Markov. He's a musician. He's really big in New York. He'd love you. You'd be a good pair."

"Really?" It has not been her experience that she has been a good pair.

"Yeah, really. Save yourself for someone like him."

At Christmas, Elaine invites Tracy to New York.

"My family is dying to meet you," Elaine says on the phone. "They all ask, 'When is Tracy coming?'"

From the airport, Tracy takes a bus to Port Authority. She carries an Army duffel bag and wears her ostrich skin dress boots, her only protection in the city where she is street-stupid. The noise and confusion of the terminal make her skin hurt and her chest muscles contract. She heads into the bright fuzzy winter light toward the building where she is to meet Elaine for an office party at five. She walks a few blocks the wrong way before she figures out Elaine's instructions. She arrives early, takes the elevator up, then stands in the lobby with her bag between her boots while people in business suits walk past staring at her.

At five-thirty, Elaine shows up wearing a short white fake-fur coat and a black stretch miniskirt, looking thinner and more disconcerting than ever.

"Tracy! How are you? Are you having a good time? Could you follow my directions? I wrote them so queerly." She laughs. "Come on. I'll introduce you to *everyone*."

Elaine tows Tracy around the reception area introducing her as an artist from out west. People admire her silver and copper jewelry, which she made, and ask how she likes Los Angeles. Tracy gives her name, which Elaine consistently forgets to do, and tells them she lives in Santa Fe. Finally, Elaine parks her by the food.

"I know you like to eat," Elaine says.

Tracy is hungry, so she eats. She notices the other women either clutch drinks or pass food, but they do not eat. The men eat, so Tracy's position is convenient for talking with them. Soon three are gathered around her, sporting earrings, Christmas sweaters, and hiking boots, all fascinated by her descriptions of pole bending, barrel racing, spring round-ups, and mutton stew. One of them, Tom, says he might go to New Mexico for a project and gives her his card. The other men get out their cards.

Tom asks what she is doing later. Elaine says they have to leave. Tracy waves goodbye with one hand, clutching the cards in the other. In the elevator, she shows them to Elaine who says, "People in New York give each other cards all the time. It doesn't mean anything. Just throw them away."

Tracy puts them in her pocket. Outside, Elaine walks so fast that Tracy, lugging her duffel bag and disoriented by the traffic, can't keep up and almost misses the bus Elaine vanishes into. On the bus, Tracy tries to start a conversation, but Elaine wants to be left alone.

They get off in a neighborhood of rundown apartments and abandoned buildings. Tracy can't tell east from west or north from south. Elaine walks ahead then stops at a boarded-up housefront and pushes the button. Tracy catches up before the door opens. The sign beneath the buzzer says "J. Markov."

Tracy looks at Elaine. J. Markov opens the door. He is tall and slender with slack black hair and a pale intelligent face.

"Elaine! I thought you'd never get here," he says as he scoops her up.

"Julian!" she says, throwing her arms around his neck.

Tracy watches Elaine swing back and forth in the air as Julian's large talented hands curve around her butt. She has no idea why Elaine has invited her here.

"My friend Tracy wants to meet you," Elaine says, twisting in Julian's arms and pointing to Tracy as her feet touch the ground.

Julian and Tracy nod at each other.

"Come in," he says. He wraps his arm around Elaine's shoulders, escorting her.

Tracy follows. She would prefer to walk away, but she doesn't know where she is. She sits on the couch. On the rug covering part of the cement floor is a saxophone in its open case, a music stand, and scattered sheets of music. Julian brings out wine and puts on slow sexy jazz. Elaine takes his hand. They dance, Elaine twirling away from him then rubbing herself against his thigh.

When Elaine's skirt is to her waist, Tracy gets up and uses the bathroom. When she comes out, Julian and Elaine are lying on the rug intertwined. She walks out the door and closes it. She intends to get a cab then realizes she doesn't know Elaine's address and doesn't have a key. She looks up and down the street and tries not to cry. She will have to buzz J. Markov and get Elaine to help her.

Elaine laughs when she sees Tracy standing at the door.

"I just want to go home," Tracy says.

"No." Elaine laughs again.

Julian comes to the door. "Come in, Tracy."

"No. I want to go home."

"Well, you can't," Elaine says. "So you have to come in."

Tracy is mad. "Tell me where I am. Tell me how to get home. Give me your keys."

"Don't be so upset. We were all having a nice time."

"Come in," Julian repeats.

Tracy steps inside. "Would you please call a taxi," she tells Julian, surprised at herself. She has never ordered a taxi. "Please tell him how to get here."

"Oh, all right," Elaine concedes. "Would you make the call, Julian."

While Julian calls, Tracy and Elaine sit at opposite ends of the couch. Julian comes in and sits by Elaine. She runs her black-stockinged toe up and down the calf of his blue jeans. They kiss. After a few minutes, Tracy walks outside.

In the cab, she starts crying. She doesn't know what to do. Tomorrow she could be having Christmas Eve dinner with Elaine's family or pretzels on a plane. She has talked to Elaine's mother on the phone. She sounds comforting and sweet.

With hands as insubstantial as ghosts, Tracy manages to get through a series of locks into the small studio apartment. She is almost asleep in the loft when she hears a buzzer go off. She doesn't know what it is. It buzzes again. She turns on the light and walks to the door where she notices an intercom. She presses buttons until she hears Elaine's voice.

"Let me in."

It occurs to her not to; then, she can't figure out how to. Elaine has to tell her what to do. Tracy gets back into bed and pretends to sleep. Why Elaine would cut short a night with Julian Markov, she can't comprehend.

Elaine enters and makes elaborately quiet and prolonged preparations for bed. As she turns off the light she tells Tracy, "I hate to talk in the morning, so please don't talk to me."

Okay, Tracy thinks. *That'll be easy.*

In the morning Tracy wakes up when she hears Elaine on the phone talking about her evening. Tracy dresses, packs, then sits on the futon beneath the loft.

When Elaine gets off the phone she says, "I don't know why you left last night, but it wasn't my fault."

"I was tired. I just wanted to go to sleep. That's all."

Elaine looks defiant. "You have no right to judge my sexual behavior."

It's the greatest anomaly yet

"I don't care what you do," Tracy answers. "I just don't want to have to watch."

"Well, I'm trying to show you a good time, but if you're not happy, I guess you may as well go home."

"I guess so."

Elaine puts on her coat. "I've only got one set of keys, so if you go, you can't get back in. I'll be back around five. Do whatever you have to do."

Tracy nods. Elaine yanks the door open and leaves, the injured party.

Tracy goes to the refrigerator and takes out a carton of milk, the only thing in it. She pours herself a glass, sits at the table, then pulls Tom's card out of her back pocket and turns it between her fingers. From now on, she tells herself, she's going to have to pay attention to what is really going on.

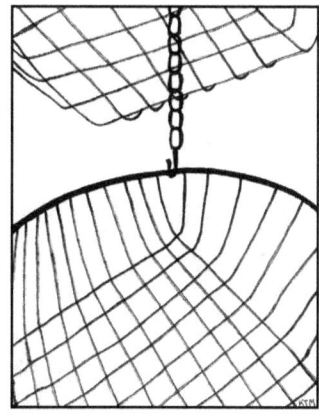

Red Boots

MY FRIEND CHRISTINE IS dramatically good-looking with ivory skin, a regal hooked nose, and a cloud of black curls floating down her back. I'm rosy-cheeked and brown-haired with some sort of comforting appeal. We work in the merchandising office of a department store in downtown New York. Christine orders shoes for the entire chain. I carry things for people and compliment them a lot.

About the only thing we have in common is her husband, Philip, who's so gorgeous we just try to ignore him. He's got the easy confidence that comes from being large and athletic— good-looking in a smooth predatory way—a six-foot four-inch hunk of male meat. When he comes into a room and sees something he likes, his blue eyes light up, he smiles, and takes over. Always going for the goodies, that's how I think of him. And when you're the goodies, it's great. He and Christine survey everything like two superior birds—hawks.

When people see the three of us, they call me over and say, "Who's that fabulous woman you're with? And who's that terrific guy? They look so great together."

"They are," I always say, and I always tell Christine.

Only once did someone call me over and say, "Who's that couple you're with? They look so incompatible, like they don't fit together."

"They don't," I said, because like everything else, this is also true. I didn't tell Christine though.

In exchange for babysitting their five-year-old son, Victor, Christine gives me the necklace she got from the boyfriend who hooked her on throwing the *I Ching*. It's a round crystal the size of a marble suspended in the claws of a silver bird's foot. Christine says she knows it isn't my style, but it will bring me luck. I hang it in my kitchen window hoping my life will become like hers: charmed.

Saturday night they take me dancing. I spend the evening twirling sugar beads on an elastic string around my neck while Christine and Philip twirl around the dance floor. I chew the yellow candies first, then the orange, then the red, leaving the green for last. A man watches. He isn't good-looking. He's scraggly, middle-aged.

Finally, he comes up to me. "Please, I just want to suck on those candies around your neck." He strokes the air by my face.

"No," I say, closing my hands around them.

"I just wanna, I just wanna feel those candies in my mouth." He puts his fingers between his lips and touches the tip of his tongue.

Luckily, Christine and Philip come up, and the guy goes away.

The next day I'm standing in their kitchen waiting for Christine to get Victor ready so we can all go to the park. Philip comes in looking for Christine's shoe. Christine always has great shoes, nothing flat or clunky—high-heeled boots or sandals for casual, strappy or glittery high heels for dressing up—always sleek and tight in a sexy way, like uptight, like a cat on its toes.

Philip is wearing his blue jeans and the blue-violet polo shirt that matches his eyes. It just kills me the way it stretches against his chest and around his biceps. He's looking around the toaster oven and the Cuisinart, adjusting the decorative piles of vegetables and fruits. Every move he makes is so confident, so purposeful, like he's three-dimensional and the rest of the world is two.

"Why would Christine's shoe be in the kitchen?" I ask, figuring Christine told him to find it and he didn't know where to look.

"I had it in here," he answers, lifting the rack of drying dishes.

"Why did you have her shoe in the kitchen?" I try to think of some good reason. Maybe he was studying her size to get her another pair.

He turns to me and smiles. "Because I like her shoes. I have a shoe fetish."

I laugh, but all of a sudden I know something I'd rather I didn't. It would be different if Christine had told me, but she wouldn't. She likes to keep their private life private. It makes it more exciting for her.

Philip finds her shoe in the hanging basket of oranges. This particular model is clear plastic with black and copper cords crisscrossing all the way above the ankle. He takes it out of the room, stroking it. I stay in the kitchen waiting for something to happen, but something already has.

A few weeks later Christine invites me to the Halloween party she and Philip are having. I have to get an outfit. In the window of my favorite thrift store I see a pair of women's red leather cowboy boots. I can't believe how beautiful they are—new and shiny with gold and silver details. I go in thinking the boots must be part of a display, they can't be for sale, they can't be my size, I can't afford them. I ask to try them on. Fifty bucks, size nine, they fit perfectly.

The manager of the thrift store tells me the woman who brought them in on consignment is a compulsive shopper. The boots are one year old and have never been worn. They still have the original price tag, $250. They are a designer label. I can imagine seeing them on the cover of *ELLE* magazine, they are at least that good.

I can't wait to show them to Christine and Philip. I know they will love them. I know they will love them as much as I love them. I know Christine and I both wear a size nine. I know they would look great with the skintight black jeans she likes to wear. I rub the pointy toes and high wooden heels then put the boots back in their box.

For the party I wear a black miniskirt and a red midriff top with the boots. I arrive early. Philip smiles when he opens the door.

The boots echo as I cross the hardwood floor of their living room. The expression "to die for" goes through my head. I get a rush from it.

"Oh, those boots. They're just to die for," Christine says as I walk into the kitchen.

We look at each other, our power reversed. I'm the one who always envies her. I smile and keep walking toward her, but she sticks out her long thin arm to keep me away.

I stop and look down at my boots. The shiny red toes curl up at me like the muzzles of two six-guns, like the tips of two bright red fingernails, like two red-sequined nipples, like everything sexual that can be bought for fifty dollars. They are to die for.

Philip looks me up and down, walking around me so he can see better. Christine hasn't moved.

"Nice," Philip says. "Very nice."

I turn my hands out, stare at the red pointy toes, and say something vacuous.

"Why don't you give those to Christine?" His eyes shift between her and the boots.

I smile at him and don't answer, thinking he's just flattering me.

The guests begin arriving. I serve the hors d'oeuvres so Christine and Philip can be the center of attention. But all night, whenever I cross through the living room, everyone knows whose feet the red boots are on.

When everyone goes home, the three of us gather in the kitchen. I offer to leave the boots for the night.

"You guys can enjoy them," I say.

Philip puts his arm around Christine's shoulder. He smiles. She looks distressed.

I pull the first boot off. "Be careful. Don't scratch them."

She says, "No. Don't leave them if you want them back."

"You're kidding," I say. "Of course I want them back, but you can borrow them. Go ahead. I want you to use them." I get a rush thinking of them having a good time.

"I'm warning you," she says. "Don't leave them if you want them. Take them with you unless you want to give them to me."

I look at her. I have never had anyone warn me not to loan them something. It doesn't register. I pull the second boot off. "No, I'll leave them. I don't mind. Philip wants me to leave them, so I will."

The boots are on the floor. Philip picks one up. It grows small and intimate in his large hand.

"Thanks," he says. "Goodnight."

Christine looks at me, then the boots, then Philip. I leave in the tennis shoes I walked here in.

At work Christine hands me a check for $50 marked "Paid in Full." I hand it back and ask for the boots. She shakes her head, backing away.

I spend the next two weeks looking in every store I can for another pair of boots I like better. There's nothing. I realize how great the boots are and how much I want them. By then Christine has stopped speaking to me, and I've arranged to work in another area.

Philip calls me at home. Philip has never called me before.

"Let us keep the boots," he says. "I'll give you a hundred dollars. Christine wants the boots."

"It's not the money," I say. "I want the boots."

It kills me to disappoint him, it kills me that he only called because he doesn't want Christine to be unhappy not because he cares about me, and it kills me that no matter what I do, my relationship with them will never be the same.

I have long discussions with people about friendships, possessions, and the rights and responsibilities of hosts and guests. *Do I owe Christine and Philip the boots?* They have always been generous to me, inviting me for dinner, taking me out, giving me more than fifty dollars' worth of food.

One Saturday afternoon I go to their apartment to get the boots. Victor opens the door and invites me in. Philip, Christine, and one of her friends from work, Jolene, are talking in the living room. Jolene says hello to me. It would be awkward if Christine and Philip forced me out, but I'm pretty sure that's what they want to do.

Christine walks over, hugs me as if everything's normal, and tells me how much she loves the boots. "You have to let me keep them," she says.

Philip asks, "Did you come to tell Christine she could have the boots?"

"No," I say. "I came to get the boots. Where are they? They're mine."

"But you said I could have them," Christine says.

"No, I didn't. I said you could borrow them."

"I gave you a check for them."

"I gave it back."

"I'm not giving them to you. You left them. They're mine."

"I'm sorry I left them here. I'm sorry about all of this, but I want my boots."

Victor runs toward his bedroom. Philip, Christine, and Jolene follow him, leaving me alone in the living room. I can't believe this is happening. I decide to go to Christine's closet and take the boots.

I'm terrified walking into Christine and Philip's bedroom. It's like violating sacred ground. They're the sexiest couple I know, and here's their bed, rumpled and unmade. Their clothes are where they threw them. I open the huge double closet and go through piles of clothes on the floor. I can't find the boots.

I go back into the living room. I can't believe how much I am shaking, and I can't believe I am going through with this. I can't believe I don't just go home. They come back in.

"I want my boots," I say to Philip, hoping he will take my side. Instead, he and Jolene lead Victor out the front door. It's just me and Christine now.

She starts screaming. I keep listening for her to say something about us being friends, but she doesn't.

"They're not yours. They're mine. You know it. Give them to me," I say calmly.

She keeps screaming.

I say, "You have everything—Philip, Victor, your career, this apartment. Let me at least have the boots."

For some reason, this makes her really mad. She glares at me so intensely I almost laugh.

"I'm not leaving until I get the boots," I say, realizing I have come too far not to mean it.

She screams some more then leaves the room. I stare out the window feeling like some large tacky statue from a garage sale. Will Philip and Jolene come back and find me here? Will they start making dinner? What about breakfast in the morning?

Christine returns holding the boots upside down, the sharp points of the toes aimed like weapons at my face. At first I'm glad to see the boots; then, I realize she's going to throw them at me.

"I hope they hurt!" she screams, hurtling them one at a time.

I catch them in the air and hug them to my chest.

"I'm sorry," I say once more and leave.

I'd imagined Christine would curse the boots so I'd have an accident before I could get them or so I'd have an accident while wearing them, but the curse is only that they'll be too uncomfortable to enjoy.

I wear the boots once, to the store's Christmas fashion show. They're a great success, but I keep thinking I'll see Christine and Philip and want to hide. When I get home, I put the boots back in the box and set them outside by the trash. The next morning they're gone. I can't take down the necklace Christine gave me though. It reminds me of when we were friends.

I fantasize they'll get divorced over the whole thing and Philip will apologize to me, but weeks later, as I leave work in the snow, I see Christine standing at a stop light with Philip and Victor, the three of them huddled together at the edge of a crowd. They look so vulnerable, like refugees from some frozen fallen city. Who else besides me knows who they are or cares? Yet looking back, I realize I was never quite comfortable with them. I was always nervous, and I never knew quite why or how to break away.

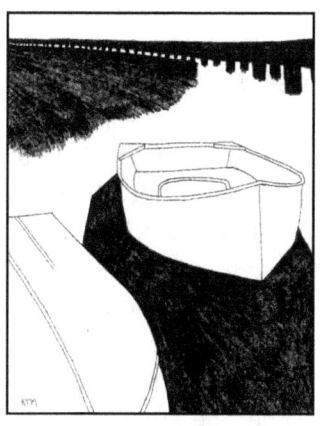

Any Failure to Obey Orders Will Be Considered an Act of Aggression

—paraphrased from *Thelma and Louise*

THE PEST CONTROL MAN COMES for the second time in a month to spray Candy's house, only now the roof is torn off and the two-by-fours are exposed because of the damage the termites have done. Standing on her lawn, twisting her kinky yellow hair, Candy stares at the little cottage, wildly overpriced because of its location in this colorful Cape Cod town, and recently abandoned to her by her fiancé. Its four walls rise like a temple to the sky.

She asks how much to write the check for.

"Nothing," the pest control man, who is married, says suggestively. He's swarthy and handsome in a French way except for the moles on his eyelids like tiny white beads. He'll be back when the house is finished to say hello he promises as he walks away.

Candy returns to the bedroom where a few minutes before she and the pest control man kissed, his tongue fat and wet in her mouth long after she wanted it there. She continues to scrub wallpaper paste off the bedroom wall, embarrassed to tell her lesbian carpenters she just got her house sprayed for free. She is stripping the wallpaper because some of the drywall is rotten and has to be replaced.

She's waiting for Rory, her boyfriend, sort of, to bring back a book she loaned him. She's giving him his sunglasses, a picture she drew for him, and a bottle of sunscreen she bought because she worries about all the sun he gets on his fair Irish face. Rory is forty-four or forty-five and needs to be careful about getting skin cancer, she's afraid. He's afraid of looking old and keeps going in the sun to bring the bloom back to his cheeks. He keeps a box of Miss Clairol blonde in his closet. When he lies back in bed, his hair falls so to reveal his gray roots. Last week he saw it in her eyes when she saw the gray roots. This is the kind of thing she does to people, expose their deepest secrets. It's a terrible habit and makes her not want to have any friends.

After she exposed his gray roots, Rory started withdrawing from her, and she got angry and started breaking up with him. All week she's been telling people Rory is breaking up with her, but this morning, in a moment of sanity, she realized that every time she called he said everything was fine. She's the one who's freaking out. That was the note she left him yesterday: "I am freaking out."

He called like she asked and said in a light hopeful voice, "Everything's fine, honey. I'd tell you if anything was wrong."

He has called her "honey" from the night they met in the bar where he works. She was engaged at the time. He was just divorced.

Rory is the consummate bartender, quick and well-defended, a neat little package of bulging arms and tight hips. "Give us a spin, Rory," Candy hears the younger women say. They want to check him out. He won't do it right then when they ask for it, but all night as he paces behind the counter he does, turning smoothly on his toes. In his precise white pants and tight-chested T-shirts, Rory looks like he was in the Navy, and he was.

She loves it when Rory calls her "honey." Her father called her that in the same sweet protective tone: "Goodnight, honey." "Everything's fine, honey." But now her father is dead. After he died, her fiancé moved out. He and her father had more in common than he and she did.

Waiting for Rory to arrive so she can break up with him, Candy gets so angry she has to leave the house. She goes to the grocery store to buy peaches and lettuce. That's what she has been living on lately along with people's leftovers from the restaurant where she works.

"Are you eating well?" her convention-bound mother asks on the phone.

"Yes," she answers. "Lots of fruits and vegetables."

Outside the store she runs into a friend. Unemployed, the friend is studying to be a proofreader.

"I can stay home with the kids and do it by email the rest of my life, as long as my eyesight doesn't go," she explains. She already has a permanently damaged shoulder from being a waitress and a masseuse.

Since being laid off from her social worker job because of cutbacks in government services, Candy works nights busing tables and days as a maid, taking the positions of people she might have previously helped. Because she was left with the loan on the house, she is one hundred thousand dollars in debt.

"The problems of the rich are not as serious as the problems of the poor," her mother expounds, sounding like someone in *The Great Gatsby.*

"At least you own your own home," everyone assures her.

She would make more money being a waitress, but her middle-class parents raised her to believe she was better than that, so she has no experience. Some mornings she cleans the toilets for the same people she cleaned the table for the night before. She tries not to think about how intimately she is connected to the digestive cycle.

Lately she's been thinking about having a baby for some wealthy couple, using her uterus to hold their sperm and egg. She figures she could get ten thousand dollars, the price of the repairs to her house. She figures she'd better make a decision soon before she gets any older, and before some group has it outlawed so women such as herself are spared the tragedy of having to sell their reproductive services.

Candy has been getting more hours at the motel because another maid, Trisha, who is twenty, a perky little redhead, round and compact like a top, was first pregnant by one of her two boyfriends then miscarried. Candy's glad she's over thirty and smart enough to be on the Pill, but she feels ruthless getting more money while Trisha lies at home bleeding, uninsured, unemployed. Rory says not to worry. Life is tough.

Candy and her friend watch a woman trying to get her rusted-out car into reverse. It grinds horribly each time she tries then won't catch.

Candy is afraid the woman is going to hit her car. She screams "WATCH OUT!" The poor woman looks up in fright, her car stalling and rolling.

Candy feels like a fish in the ocean—eat or be eaten, catch or be caught. The economy is reducing them all to predators again. She believes by the time she dies, America will be like a third-world country ruled by a few lily-fingered men growing demented with wealth. She was raised to have her worst nightmare be to live in a third-world country.

"Aren't we lucky to live in America?" her mother frequently asks.

While she was at the store, Rory came by, her carpenters tell her. He picked up his stuff and left hers.

Good, that's over, she thinks as she returns to stripping the wallpaper in the aquatic light created by the blue plastic tarp the carpenters have spread over the roofless frame of her house. At least eventually she thinks that, once she gets over feeling depressed, then angry, then thinking how like them it is to misconnect. Before they started going together, they ran into each other nearly every day. Now she hasn't seen him for a week. Other guys come on to her all the time, like the pest control man.

At first she and Rory went for bike rides and walks along the beach. She knew it looked picturesque—the two of them fit, sunny-haired, windswept—but she was bored, and Rory, insecure, never said a kind word, tested her with stupid jokes like a kid would: "How do you tell a gerbil from a hamster? A hamster has more dark meat." When she told him how cute he was, he would cringe, visibly.

Rory's mother died of MS when he was eleven. His father died of a heart attack when he was sixteen. His older sister took care of him until he enlisted at eighteen. The Navy took care of him while he drank. At twenty-six, he got married. Now Rory takes care of his son who is turning sixteen. Rory is having a hard time staying close to him now that he has reached the age Rory was when both of his parents were dead.

That night Candy works at the restaurant. Bob, the host, who is good-looking but not bright, is jealous of her because the rich old men want to talk to her and hold her hand, which she lets them do. She hopes one of them will give her a job, elevate her to the level of manager somewhere, like Bob is, like she used to be. Bob wishes the rich old men would hold his hand and flirt with him. Bob is married and a closet queen. It's the fact that he's in the closet and has to lay next to his wife in their dark bed that makes him so mean, Candy tells herself, trying to feel sympathy for him when what she would like to do is pound his dull-witted face.

She and Bob glare at each other. Frequently, he refuses to return her greeting, and again tonight he walks right by when she says hello. But when it gets busy they work in tandem to please the owner, Louie. Everyone wants to please Louie. He is Big Daddy and makes the decisions that support them. All of his employees are gay men or attractive straight females or related to him by marriage or birth.

Her first night busing, after five hours she sat at an empty booth near the busing station. Bob came over and told her Louie, whom she was looking at, had seen her, and she was never to do that again. She couldn't believe that for minimum wage she was not allowed to sit once in an eight-hour shift. You have to be making much more to sit around like she used to. When she goes to the state employment office looking for a better job, the people working there seem to do nothing but sit around, exchanging recipes, talking about television shows and bargains at the A & P. When other clients have trouble accessing the job listings, they turn to her for help.

Her fellow busperson, Marvin, a gay queen, willowy—unlike Bob who is built like a brick—drops a tray of dishes nearly every night. Never in the history of the restaurant have so many dishes been broken. He argues with the waiters about what he is and isn't supposed to do. No one likes him, but Louie won't fire anyone who keeps showing up. Since they started work, Candy has been Marvin's only friend. Many times she has scooped up plates for him just before they fell or interceded in other ways.

So far she has dropped one tray. A few weeks ago when one of the waiters, Paul, was casually turning around during a rush with his empty tray floating in his hand he caught her in the face with the edge of it, right between her lip and her nose. She thought she could keep moving, but the tray seemed to stick to her face as if Paul were holding it tight, and maybe he was.

When she realized she was going to fall, and that her tray was going to fall first, rather than landing in the broken dishes on her face, she decided to let go of her tray and use her hands to break her fall. Since all of this happened rather slowly, and she is noticeably long-legged and conspicuous, she was aware that the whole dining room was turned to look at her. With one forearm she braced herself against a wall that stopped her momentum but caused deep bruises where her skin pressed into a decorative horseshoe. The tray crashed, spraying glass everywhere, but she managed to recover herself before she hit the ground. All around her people were laughing. It didn't seem that funny to her.

She paused to look at the damage. Ferret-like Marvin, Bob—raging—and the waiters moved in for the cleanup. She walked into the kitchen to get the broom and gather herself. When she came out, Marvin, as usual, was crouched in the middle of a pile of glass. She told him to get up and started sweeping. She reached in to salvage unbroken bowls and cups, but her fingers started stinging with glass so she stopped. She swept up everything and carried it to the kitchen trash. The headwaiter spotted unbroken dishes in the can and started picking them out, his job being to serve Louie in any way, but Candy, with glass-cut fingers, a bruised forearm, and her face throbbing from the tray hitting above her lip, didn't offer to help him. He looked at her and didn't ask.

Paul, who was supposedly her friend, never apologized or offered to help. He just disappeared. Later he advised her if she ever dropped a tray again to do the same. "Let someone else clean it up," he said.

Afterward she started to bus a table, but when she picked up an empty salad bowl and the man at the table told her to put it down, she went to the bathroom to compose herself. She wanted to call Rory when she got home, maybe go to his house, but he didn't get off work until at least two; then, he liked to be left alone to sleep until about four the next afternoon when he got up to work again.

Tonight her night is going smoothly. The customers are friendly and some of her favorite waiters are on. She tries to ignore Marvin who complains when the customers want to take their food home because then he can't eat it: "I suppose they're not going to leave those shrimp," he whines, touching them in their bowl on Candy's tray. And he complains when customers leave their food behind: "I wish I had that kind of money to throw away on food, don't you?"

They are standing in the kitchen, their trays on the busing rack, sorting their dishes for the dishwasher, and Marvin says, "I wish they'd get this place organized. I don't see how they expect us to work here."

Candy tries to block him out. The restaurant has been in business for forty years and seems adequately run to her. She is staring at her tray, arguing with Marvin in her mind, when Louie walks into the kitchen. She looks up, and somehow, inexplicably, her tray falls to the floor the moment he walks by. Plates and glasses crash.

Everyone thinks Marvin has dropped them, and Louie shouts, "Marvin, the next tray you drop, you're paying for!"

"It was my tray," Candy says, being noble, and, knowing her own innocent history, thinks Louie will tell her it's okay.

"The next tray you drop, Candy, you pay for!" Louie says and walks out.

"Don't talk to me anymore," she tells Marvin, calculating

that each dropped tray could cost a whole night's tips, making her job so unprofitable she might have to quit.

Marvin, in his prissiest voice, says, "It wasn't my fault you dropped the damn tray."

Now she'll have to deal with him all night unless she can smooth it over.

"I know it wasn't your fault, but I can't talk and work at the same time. Could you please not talk to me," she says. "And please don't be mad."

"I'm not mad," Marvin snips. "I don't have a problem. You have the problem. You dropped the tray."

"Louie doesn't see people, he just sees dollar signs," D. J., the black dishwasher, remarks. Like most everybody at the restaurant, he has worked for Louie for years.

For the rest of the night she glares when she sees Louie laughing with the waiters and the customers. She knows he won't apologize. He's probably forgotten the whole incident. *Louie doesn't see people, just dollar signs.* She decides that for the night she doesn't have to be nice. She takes the bowls and plates without smiling. She makes everyone well aware of her mental state.

One of the waiters, Tony, who didn't see her spill the tray in the kitchen, asks her, in his rich Virginia accent, "You okay, hon-ney?"

She has come to work with migraines and menstrual cramps, after six hours of being a maid, and with swollen legs and feet. This is the first time anyone has seriously asked her if she's okay. As she looks at him, she gives in to all the pity she feels for herself. She can't answer, but mercifully she turns away before she starts to cry.

"You don't bring your problems to the station," her fiancé, a fireman, told her. He worked cooped up with seven other men for forty-eight hours at a time. *You don't bring your problems to the station.*

"I'm fine, thanks," she tells Tony later. "Thanks for asking." She pats him on the back, and he smiles at her.

At the end of the night, Bob hands her her share of the tips without comment. He thanks the waiters who have done half as much work and made twice the money.

"Goodnight, *gentlemen,*" Bob says.

Louie smiles, and they depart, Candy to her roofless house that the carpenters have ordered her not to stay in because there is plaster dust and sawdust everywhere. She lies down to sleep in her clothes on the plastic tarp covering the floor. She's sure she has seen this done somewhere, maybe in a situation comedy about newlyweds. Just last week Rory said she could stay with him any time she needed to.

The next morning at the motel Candy learns that a grandmother traveling with her family died in her bed during the night. Candy stands outside their suite. Lucinda, the Portuguese maid who speaks no English and doesn't know what happened, rushes around trying to clean it while the family is still gathering their things. The owner yells at Lucinda.

Later Candy finds her sitting on the steps crying. Lucinda doesn't understand why they're mad at her. Normally, she does good work and is proud to be the fastest maid.

Candy sits down and pats her back. Earlier Candy patted the woman whose mother had died.

I'm only in it for the money, Lucinda indicates to Candy, rubbing her thumb and two fingers together to show cash, tears in her eyes.

"I know," Candy says, though she knows Lucinda loves her job.

After the family is gone, Candy and the other maids stand in the room eating the food left behind. They don't get a lunch break, so they're starving. Even though the old woman died peacefully in her sleep, this is probably what everyone fears, Candy thinks while eating a donut meant for the family's breakfast. The woman's body has been taken away by ambulance men who made jokes in the parking lot while the police questioned the family, the bed has been stripped, ready to be remade, the handyman sings as he puts his share of the spoils in a plastic bag. Candy and the other maids rush through their food so the motel owner doesn't catch them and shout at them, making a fool of himself in front of the guests.

When she gets home, Candy has a message on her machine from the pest control man. He wants her to work with him, an easy job, nine dollars an hour, cash. He could pick her up at 8 a.m. She'd be done by four.

"I'd like to *have* you," he says.

She doesn't want it to be like this. She sees herself in a dark empty building, trapped with him, her shouts echoing against bare walls. She would like to call Rory and ask what to do, but she's embarrassed by the situation. Anyway, she and Rory don't seem to be speaking. But she needs the money, and she has the day off.

She leaves a message that she'll do it. The law is on her side, she tells herself. People can't just do whatever they want to you.

Hot Ticket to Nowhere

I'VE BEEN LOOKING AT WEDDING rings a lot lately—on fingers—not in stores. I think they tell a lot about a man. My friend Alan's ring is wide rounded gold. It sits enshrined on his fat white finger. We are lawyers for the same firm in this Connecticut town.

After work I flop down in his office chair and notice an invitation on his desk for a dinner party given by the mayor. It is addressed to "Mr. and Mrs." I complain about my empty social agenda.

"Women are everywhere," he says. "They're desperate. I bet if I weren't married, I could have a date every night with a reasonably bright, reasonably attractive woman. Face it, a man who is a lawyer or a doctor isn't going to have any problem getting a woman."

Alan's wife comes in. She is crying and panicked like a child with her bobbed hair, round collar, and wrap skirt. She is thin but not in a seductive way. Alan married her, he says, because he felt sorry for her, and she was a nice girl, a virgin until the end—their wedding night. She is crying because she bumped someone in a parking lot with their car. She is crying because she wasn't sure how to do both the legal and the moral thing. If she errs in either direction, Alan is sure to catch and punish her.

"I wanted to leave a note," Pam says between huge sobs and gulps of air. "But I was afraid he might accuse me of doing something I didn't do. I couldn't find any marks on the car, but it didn't seem right to drive away. I got his license plate so you could tell me what to do."

Alan tells her what to do, beginning with how to breathe so she'll stop crying in his office.

I get my dark blonde hair clipped concentration-camp style. My face feels light and bony in my hands. I have a date with a real estate agent whose name is on signs all over town. He is good-looking and confident but not my age. He is some older age. There is gray in his thinning brown hair.

But this is what every girl wants, I think Alan would say as my date stands ominously in my doorway. What is he an omen of? Of everything that went wrong with free love and be-ins. His life is a pastiche of clichés. We are going to a health food restaurant in his fancy red sports car that he drives fast. I lean back in the seat and shut my eyes. I am good at making conversation, that is how I get these dates, so I make some. It's about this car, other cars, this road, other roads. I make a net out of air, not so much to catch him as to catch myself, but we both are caught.

At dinner I notice the gold band, and by looking at my left hand figure out that it is on his right hand. I realize when he talks about his wife he does not say he is divorced.

"That's a funny thing to wear on a date," I say.

He laughs and smiles at me. I am so clever.

"I wear it for her," he says. "It helps her."

I ask him how.

"She needs me. We still see a lot of each other. I moved it to the other hand when we separated about five years ago. When we get divorced, I guess I'll take it off."

What a hero, I think. Getting divorced might help her more.

I am sitting in Alan's office telling him about my date. "Men are desperate. They'll try anything."

Alan leans back in his chair to appraise me: I don't look right, I don't dress right, my haircut was a mistake. He describes with his hands ways I could do everything differently.

He checks his watch. It is after five. His day is done. Soon Pam will be here to take him home. He smiles as he tells me that when he was in college his fraternity would pay for a bus to come from a sorority at a nearby college. It would deposit the women at the entrance of the school on Friday afternoons. The prettiest ones would be picked up quickly by the jocks and frat rats. The others would not. The bus would wait around the corner then take them back. His is an old and well-respected college. His diploma is displayed proudly on the wall. It gets him places people without it cannot go.

When we hear Pam's horn, he looks out the window and deliberately pours himself another cup of coffee. He sits back and drinks it. The office is orange with sunset and sexual tension, what with women waiting and being picked up, being chosen and not chosen, frat weekends and fast cars. Alan looks at me. He wonders what it would be like to have an affair. He wishes Pam would have an affair. Their marriage has grown dull. They haven't had sex for weeks. He's suggested she have an affair with one of the doctors at the clinic where she volunteers, but the doctors at the clinic are old and feeble, she says. She'd rather have sex at home.

This doesn't make sense to me. It's like wearing your wedding ring on a date to protect your wife. Our shoulders touch as we walk down the narrow wooden hallway. When we finally get to the car, Pam and I are embarrassed to look at each other. She's been sitting in the empty parking lot for at least a quarter hour. Alan steps into the passenger side and waves goodbye as they drive away.

There is a party given by a couple from the office. At these parties almost everyone is a couple. Inviting a single woman is like inviting an ex-wife to your wedding—a calculated act of courage. You feel nervous but big-hearted. I don't always get invited.

Joe and Lucy Martin are here. Joe is in charge of public relations. He used to be a newspaper man. He likes to bet on horses and football and tell about his adventures in the red light district. When prominent people get arrested and make the front page of the paper, he knows them. Lucy is a librarian. They invited me to dinner once. They had silver and linen, crystal and china, roast beef and mashed potatoes. I couldn't remember the last home-cooked meal I had been served. I thanked them and sent flowers afterward, but Lucy came in the office one day when Joe was flirting with me. I never got asked back.

Alan and Pam are here. Jeanette and Randy Burch are here. Randy is my age and works in my office. Jeanette is fifteen years older. I broke up with my last boyfriend on the Saturday we were supposed to go to their house for dinner. I called to say I would be a little late and alone. She said she had everything planned for four; it wouldn't work out to serve three.

"Do you mean I can't come to dinner by myself?" I said.

"No, we'll do it another time. It's so much nicer to have a foursome, don't you think? We'll talk to you later." She hung up.

Standing in the kitchen watching the couples revolve around each other, I remember that last night I dreamed I was at a party. I was telling these stories about being single. Everyone was laughing; then, they said, "You tell good stories, but they're always about how vulnerable young women are. We want to hear happy stories where women get what they want." In the dream I am left speechless. I tell the only stories I know. I don't know stories where men and women are paired fruitfully two by two on their way to the Ark. I look around the kitchen. There are couples everywhere, arguing over how to make turkey and salad and rolls. I start to back up, but I don't see anywhere to go.

In college one day we went hiking and came to a stream full of rapids, fast-moving, too wide to get across. We stripped down to our bathing suits. I thought we all wanted to swim, but my friends only put their feet in the water. I stepped into the stream and lay on my back, as if on an inner tube, prepared to ride the rapids. I wished there were inner tubes, I wished we all had them, but we didn't. I couldn't let that stop me, so I imagined having one and did without.

By arching my back I could float and drift slowly through the shallow water; then, the stream narrowed and plunged between two boulders. I threw one hand over my head, threw my head back, and trusted the water. It arched me over the rocks and pulled me down into the whirlpool, pounded on me, then shot me up again.

I smiled at my friends on the side then stiffened my body and guided it like a boat through more boulders and was pulled over the rocks to the bottom of a four-foot drop and shoved out again, this time into a quiet pool where I could swim.

I wanted everyone to ride with me, and one guy tried it, but he got scared: Instead of opening his body up so it would float, he closed in on himself and sunk, dropping over a cascade to the bottom, held down until someone pulled him out.

I realized none of them understood what I did as I went through those rapids, sometimes getting turned around and going through backward or face-first, each time coming out more scratched and sore until at the end my friends started seeing bruises all over my numb body and made me stop.

The rapids were saying to me, *This is your life. This is what it feels like. This is practice on how to survive.* I can still feel the suck and crash as I arched my back and was pulled under. I can see the sky above the white water pounding on my face. I tell myself *I don't need to breathe. I live in this world like a giant charmed fish. I can wait forever to be pushed back into the open air.* Then I pop up, and for a moment I can breathe before going down again.

I attend a conference on women, public policy, and the law because our office considers itself socially progressive. The conference is in a New York hotel for three days. There are men there. I had forgotten there would be.

"There are four sentences to remember when anyone says everything is equal now," the keynote speaker, a woman, says. "Women make up one-half of the world's population. Women do three-quarters of the world's work. Women earn one-third of the world's income. Women own one-twentieth of the world's property." I put this in my notes.

At the break I talk to Rachel, an investment counselor from Boston who's even younger than I am, slim and pretty with wild brown hair cut neatly off at chin-level, wearing a wool suit and looking like the kind of woman I've seen only in advertisements. By the time she explains how she's made herself the expert on socially responsible investing in her office, a position she's glad to hold for many reasons, I wish she were my sister instead of a person I may never see again.

A good-looking man with short dark hair and suntanned wrinkles around his blue eyes has been listening to her and introduces himself as Matt. His easy smile widens to include me. He's from a law office in New Jersey. We swap legal battle horror stories: a woman thrown into jail twice for refusing to face her rapist in court, a man losing custody of his two children when a slumlord turned off the heat. Matt wears a gold wedding band with a deep-set diamond. He turns it back and forth distractedly on his neat white hand.

Dana, hunky and intense behind wire rim glasses, joins us. He is a from the legal aid department in Maine. His dark brown curly hair is sweaty and pressed close to his head. His full pouty lips are powdery white and cracked, so he keeps licking them. He's just ridden down on his motorcycle, he explains.

I ask him about his bike, and he offers to show it to me.

Another hero, another ride, I think.

Matt and Rachel discuss their impossible case loads. Dana bites his cuticles until they bleed. He is not overworked. Where he lives people shoot each other's dogs or don't let their children off their property instead of settling things in court. I tell myself he is interesting but too difficult. We leave for the next session and sit together. Dana stops the lecturer to argue. Everyone looks at him. We are supposed to be playing on the same team here.

We decide to go drinking that night. I spend a hundred dollars getting my hair shaped and lightened. I wear black pants, a red cashmere sweater, and red lipstick, bright against my pale skin, with my white-blonde hair that is now longer and feathery. We meet in the lobby. Everyone says how great I look. I haven't heard that in a long time.

Dana puts his hand on my shoulder to look at me. "I love your hair. I love your outfit. You look so beautiful tonight."

I smile and don't know how to handle this.

At a nightclub down the street we talk shop because it's all we know. I can't drink, and I can't talk shop, and I can't stop watching Dana. I start dancing and make everyone dance with me at least once. Rachel is the best dancer. She is aware of her figure and her face and her easy grace. She smiles at me, and I feel favored. Matt is too good-looking to let go in a connected way, but it is enough to watch his handsome face go through the changes in the music.

On the dance floor, Dana is into himself. He is not into the music, or the other women, or me. He is into the rough leather mud boots he brought to remind him of home. He is into scrubbing the floor with them. His worn leather jacket doesn't come off. Up close it smells of gasoline and motorcycle oil. His leather is a substitute for something, I think, but I am not sure what.

We walk back to the hotel. Matt puts one arm around Rachel's shoulder and one around mine. He smiles at us and holds out his left hand. "I've heard that some people take their wedding rings off on the way to these conferences."

"That's disgusting," Dana says.

I look up at him. He is looking straight ahead.

In the elevator Matt suggests we go to his room for a drink. This is a good suggestion, everybody thinks, better than going to bed together or alone. Matt and Rachel sit on the two chairs. I sit on the bed. Dana sits on the floor next to me. He makes his stories of Marine training camp—small boats full of men puking before diving into the ocean for their scuba test then running up and down the beach with the boat held over their heads—seem funny. But that is a hard way to get to a law office in Maine.

While Rachel and Matt talk and pour more drinks, Dana moves onto the bed. I ask him where his family is.

"I don't know. I don't keep in touch. My parents are in Europe somewhere. I have one brother in Chicago. The other one's out West. I don't like them. They don't like me."

We hold hands. I feel like we are tied to a rescue line, hauling each other in.

Dana and I leave together. In the hallway we walk along, bumping each other like high school kids. He tells me he always has trouble with women. I say he doesn't seem to be having any now. Outside my door we kiss. He is strong but distracted. His soft lips cover mine. When I stand on tiptoe, our pelvic bones meet.

"I like you," I say.

"Don't," he says. He pulls back. "Don't get involved with me. I'm a bad person. Believe me. I can't tell you why, but I am."

We kiss each other once more; then, I watch him walk down the hall.

I believe him. After all of these years I know this will be the one warning. From now on it will be all come-ons and confusion. I should stop myself, but I am in the middle of the river now. I throw my head back to watch the rocks go by.

The next day at the conference a representative from the federal government speaks. He says the government will not condone sex by paying for birth control or abortion, will not perpetuate poverty by paying for dependent children, and will not be biased in favor of special interests by allowing a child care tax credit.

"No," Dana says, standing up. "It will not be biased toward helping those who need it." He sits down.

In addition to his leather coat and boots, today he has on dark glasses. He wants to be all toughness and hard edges, but his soft baby skin and curly hair give him away. I watch him. He is very beautiful, and I want to remember what he looks like. The poor will always be with us, and so will the needs of the troubled young men.

The speaker continues. "The fortress of family life has been violated by the liberal experiments of the past decades," he says. "The Pandora of personal indulgence has to be put back into the box."

Dana shoves back his chair, making a huge noise, and in his heavy boots, leather jacket, and dark glasses, stumbles down the aisle. People push back their chairs to get out of his way. He swings out the door and is gone. It's a good thing he lives in Maine where the woods can absorb him. He would not survive too many of these New York City days with his motorcycle and his rage.

Dana is still not back when a group of us decides to go to dinner.

"I don't know what's going on with you two, but I think you're great. Don't worry about him," Matt tells me, putting his arm around me.

Why didn't I pick someone like Matt, I wonder.

Later we find Dana out dancing. We all dance together again, trading partners. I'll miss this—having people, instead of couples, in my life. I'll miss the momentum of our enthusiasm, our mass potential for success. Dana and I slow dance together. He holds me tight, and we are joined at the thigh. It is so easy to move this way. He raises his open hand, fingers spread. My hand opens to meet his.

"I think you're a hot ticket," he says.

"Thanks. So are you." Our fingers are interlaced. We are smiling at each other.

Later I suggest we all go to my room. Dana brings in a bottle of whiskey that he was going to drink alone. Matt gets ice and glasses. We flop on the beds and tell more stories until Dana passes out and Matt and Rachel leave.

I wake Dana up.

"I'm sorry," he says.

"Sorry for what?"

"I'm sorry I fell asleep. I'm sorry I'm on your bed."

"It's okay. You're okay." I wrap my arms around him. He is warm and big.

"I know you're going to hate me," he says, "but there's something I have to tell you."

"What?"

"What I meant last night. The reason you can't get involved with me."

I'm thinking he has a disease or something; then, he lets go of my hand and says, "I'm married."

"You're married?"

He's managed not to say "my wife and I" once. I was listening. I was listening to hear "we" as in "we have a dog" or "our" as in "our house," but he has monitored every noun and pronoun to create a world without people.

"You seem so lonely," I finally say.

"I am lonely."

"Why didn't you tell us? Matt told us."

He pulls away. "No. I don't want anyone to know. I have to protect my personal life. It's the most important thing to me. I have to protect my privacy."

I start to argue. Then I see his wife like a gladiator standing guard in front of his solitude. He is hiding in a cage behind. I have fought in this arena before, and I am not going to win, so I am going to make it easy for him. I am not going to tell a soul. We both move forward and we are kissing. I put my arm around his head and stroke his curly hair. With his pouting lips and big brown eyes he must have looked angelic as a child and been difficult as hell.

"I love being here with you," he says looking up at me. "When I'm at home, if my door is closed, my wife knows if she opens it I will tear her apart. She cheats on me. I'm never there for her."

I hold him tight, and his hands cover his face. He starts to cry. I tell him he has to be good to his wife if he ever wants to be happy, if he ever wants to stop tearing himself up. But he doesn't want to stop tearing himself up.

When he stops crying he says, "I shouldn't be here. My wife is going to kill me when I tell her about this."

He won't tell people that he's married, I point out, but he'll tell his wife he was with me.

"I have to," he says. He gets up and stumbles out the door.

The next morning there is one last speaker. Then the four of us have lunch. Everyone exchanges business cards and promises to keep in touch, except Dana. He says he doesn't have a card. I shrug my shoulders and pretend there's nothing between us. Maybe there is nothing between us. I can't remember what is between us, what is normal, what an affair is supposed to be like.

"Well, it's back to the wife and kids," Matt says, smiling. "I came here to get laid, but now I'm looking forward to going home for that." He knows he's lucky.

Rachel invites me to visit her in Boston. "We'll go out. We'll have a good time."

Dana is the first to go. His backpack is heavy with books he has bought.

"Let us ship them to you," I say.

"No."

Outside it is rainy and cold. The streets are greasy and slick. The highways will be a mess on a motorcycle.

"Don't leave yet. Wait and see if it clears," I beg him.

"No."

I'm crying. Rachel and Matt put their arms around my shoulders. They don't know what he is going home to.

"Take care, Dana," they say.

Dana smiles as he straps his helmet on. The weight of his backpack gathers up his jacket. He pulls his visor down. We are all getting soaked. He revs his engine. He doesn't say goodbye. He roars down the street, weaving from side to side, the tires slipping out from underneath him so every time he nearly goes down.

I cover my eyes with my hands and cry harder. I want to run after him. I want to go anywhere. I want there to be somewhere to go.

"It's okay," Matt says. "He liked you. We had a great weekend."

I put my head back and clinch my fists at my sides as I nod. I hear the rush of the wet cars and feel my body being pulled under. I reach my arms around Matt and Rachel. They put their hands on my shoulders, and I close my eyes. Ahead of me, like rapids, are more dates and more office parties, but if I stay calm I can breathe, and as I breathe I mark this place where we all stood against the river of New York traffic and promise myself to come up more often for air.

The Dangers of Disease

RIDING THE BUS OUT OF THE Vermont woods to the Boston airport, Megan puts her fingers on the window glass, framing photos of everything she passes: the curving snowy meadows, the icy roiling streams, the frozen calm of the ponds.

Arriving at Los Angeles International, she realizes she is the only person wearing pink plastic snow boots, but they are what she always wears in winter. Her mother pats her cropped hair and says she needs to do something with it. Her father looks at her boots, shakes his head, and takes her camera bag and backpack. He wants to take the camera from her neck, but she won't let him.

Megan, who is at least four inches shorter than anyone in her family, has a hard time keeping up with her father and talking to her mother while getting on the escalators and going through the automatic doors. Her mother asks how she looks, runs her hands down her silver jumpsuit, and smiles too hard. Her father looks rumpled and messy, but he doesn't seem to care. His mother is dying, which is why Megan is here.

She leaves her parents staring at the revolving luggage while she goes to the restroom. As the hot air blows on her hands in the hot stuffy bathroom, she reads, "This device has been installed for your protection to prevent the spreading of germs and the dangers of disease." She wishes she were back in Vermont peeing in the snow.

Heading north to her parents' Santa Barbara home, Porsches, BMWs, and Mercedes pass them as they speed by hill after hill flattened by terraced ranch houses. Megan asks about her grandmother.

Her father says, "She won't hardly know you. All she'll do is groan and complain."

"Now, Richard," her mother says.

Her parents tell her she's scheduled to take pictures of her brother Ron's wife, Cindi. The purpose of the pictures seems to be to capture Cindi's beauty for everyone to enjoy. Megan knows it is only her equipment her parents are asking her to use. It is not her viewpoint they want to see.

Her parents want to hear Megan is glad to be back. She knows her lack of money and a husband and a regular job cause her parents to fear for her and think she leads a limited life, when really, with their world of finances and hairdos and what the doctors say to do, she fears for them. It's hopeless. She touches her fingers to the window glass but can't find any pattern beyond her own star-shaped hand.

"Megan!" Cindi says when they come in the door.

Cindi, who is five feet ten inches, hops off the kitchen stool to greet them. She wears matching hot pink high heels, tank top, and spiral plastic earrings with her skintight blue jeans. Layers of dark brown curls engulf her shoulders and head. Megan thinks of Medusa and Samson and the power of long coiling hair; then, she hugs Cindi who towers over her.

In the dining room, Cindi shows Megan a collage she assembled from photographs Megan sent her.

"I'd like to make these for you and sell them," Cindi says. "It's fun. But Ron says it's a waste of my time. He's got better things for me to do." She smiles a big smile, the kind you'd practice in the mirror before accepting an Oscar, humble and beaming.

To photograph Cindi, Megan angles her to the sliding glass window, softening the light on her tan twenty-five-year-old face. From five feet away, it's the look every girl wants: eyes startled and alert, Arizona sunset cheeks, enticing diamond teeth.

Cindi's shoulders jut out like twisted wings. Megan doesn't

remember her being so thin, she says as she pushes Cindi's shoulders back. Cindi says she needs to gain five pounds but is too busy to eat. Megan suggests a periodic hot fudge sundae, but this isn't what Cindi wants to hear.

"Ron keeps trying to get me pregnant," Cindi says, "but I'm not ready to take care of him and a baby too. Besides, I'd kill myself if I got fat."

Megan's father, more rumpled now from taking a nap, comes in. He looks at his daughter-in-law. Cindi smiles and accepts another Oscar.

The phone rings. Megan answers it. It's Cindi's father, who started working for Ron after he lost his job, looking for Ron. Cindi's father sounds drunk. Megan doesn't know where Ron is.

Cindi's father says, "I'll find him," and hangs up.

Megan's mother comes in. "I guess he checked himself out of the clinic."

"What?"

"He's having some drinking problems. Cindi and Ron got him into one of those clinics, but they can't make him stay."

"Oh." Megan feels the way she does after being alone in the darkroom for hours then turning on the TV to see what's happening in the world and wanting to turn it off.

Cindi and Ron are on the phone about Cindi's father the rest of the afternoon, but because they believe in business as usual, they decide to go out as planned.

"There's nothing more we can do for him," Cindi says. "We've tried everything. I'm not going to let my father ruin my life."

Cindi changes her clothes repeatedly, settling on a black ruffled strapless dress, black purse, and black heels. Megan's father helps Cindi with her matching short black ruffled jacket then hugs her. Cindi walks down to her gold Corvette. They all watch her from the picture window. She waves goodbye as she steps in. This is what Megan came home for.

She goes to the bathroom to look at herself in the mirror and make sure she still exists. She has taken off her camera. It is a shield that will not work here. She sits on the toilet lid and tries to improve her fingernails by painting them dark blue. When she finishes, she thinks her hands look powerful, like the electric hands of God. She would like to be God. She would like to set things right. Then, because her father won't approve, she takes the polish off. She could defy him and go to dinner with blue fingernails, but it isn't a point worth proving, and it wouldn't be any fun. Besides, with his gray hair and formidable build, her father looks like God.

Megan goes to the kitchen to talk with her mother. Her father has gone to feed his mother at her rest home. He is used to going by himself and forgot to take Megan.

While they make dinner, her mother confides, "I just had my face lifted and my tummy tucked." She raises her chin and puts her hands on her hips to show off her new profile. "No one except your father knows. Not even Cindi and Ron. I'd die if anyone found out. It hurt like hell. But it was worth it, don't you think?"

Megan reaches for her camera, but it's not around her neck. She can't get a picture of any of this.

Her father comes home, shoving through the door and slamming it behind him. "Goddamn her!" he shouts, his fists clinched. Megan's never seen him look so big. "She's spent her whole goddamn life complaining. She's going to die complaining. God, there isn't a damn thing more I can do. I just wish she'd hurry up and die."

"She can't help it," Megan says.

"He knows that," her mother answers.

"I can't stand to listen to her complain anymore." He walks around the room then sits down. "Is dinner ready yet?"

Megan sets the table with her grandmother's china bordered with tiny yellow roses between two gold circles. It reminds Megan of the big family dinners her grandmother had in her small house when Megan was a child. Her grandmother's house has been sold, so her things are stored here.

During dinner, Megan asks why Cindi didn't go home to change.

"They're selling their house. Ron's showing it, so it's easier for her to be here," her mother says.

"Why are they selling their house? Cindi just spent a fortune decorating it."

"It was an investment. Ron sells houses. That's what we do, you know."

"Does Ron do anything besides make money?"

"Ron enjoys making money," her mother says. "It's his hobby, like some people garden or play cards."

"What does Cindi do?"

"Cindi makes people happy just by being who she is. Is there anything wrong with that?"

"I don't know," Megan admits.

When her parents talk about investing in a laundromat or a storage yard, Megan asks, "Why don't you invest in my photography career?"

"Speaking of investments," her mother says to her father, "did Ron decide to buy that airplane?"

"Yeah, I gave him a check for it," her father says.

"Did you put the amount down?"

"No, I forgot. It was sixty thousand dollars."

Her mother is disgusted. "It's not the amount. It's the fact that you forgot to write it down."

Megan agrees. It's not the amount. It's the fact that he forgot to write it down.

After dinner, Megan excuses herself and gets her camera. She wants to take pictures of everything she can—windsurfers and beach volleyball, jet skis and sea kayaks, roller blades and designer dogs. In a drawer she finds her old faded one-piece bathing suit so full of holes that the last time she wore it she was kicked out of the pool by the lifeguard. As she leaves, her mother warns her about the undertow, the transients, and the nude beach. Megan thanks her, hoping she can get pictures of it all, especially the undertow—up close in the shallow water, toes wriggling and fighting under the water and sand.

She heads toward the ocean to see what other people revere there—hang gliders and bikinis, sunglasses and plastic kites, pink palaces and customized cars. She wonders what it would be like to love what other people love—absolutely frozen faces, eyes looking nowhere like in magazines, answers stamped in bold letters. She wonders if other people are satisfied with what celebrity says, commentator prescribes, doctors discover. She wonders if they're less lonely here than she is.

She plants herself in her torn bathing suit, dirty shorts, and baseball cap on the grass near the beach and gets out her camera. Eventually, a handsome man with a dark tan, dark mustache, and bright red shorts bicycles toward her. He smiles at her. His teeth are righteously white, and in the zoom lens, for one moment, he's very close. She captures him, her picture of California. She hopes she has captured why the man makes her nervous, and why, when her parents introduce her to men like him, she makes them uncomfortable.

The sun sets at the end of a row of palm trees. Dots of light from the oil well islands sparkle like lights on a Christmas tree. The oil pumps pump away like ugly but harmless black cats crouched and eating. Megan watches the moon rise over the refinery. The pipeline gleams in the spotlights like a city that has constructed itself on another planet. She loves how peaceful and solitary it is in the dark night.

The next morning Ron and Cindi arrive during breakfast. While Ron runs along the beach, Cindi tells the story of their Saturday night. Megan's parents listen carefully.

"I hadn't eaten all day," Cindi says, smiling and waving her thin hands in the air, "and I just had two little Margaritas. Usually, I drink twice that much—not that I drink much. But before I ate, I went into the bathroom and just threw everything up. I couldn't eat after that, so me and my friend Crystal went for a walk. Crystal's dietin' anyway."

Megan's parents smile. They like how spunky Cindi is, shimmying and shaking in her bright yellow sun top and shorts, throwing back her curls and flashing her eyes, twisting on her bar stool, tearing up and holding pieces of toast so it looks like she's eating. Megan hunches over her own breakfast.

"Then we went out dancing. Ron and Crystal's date just talked and ordered shots, but Crystal and I danced our you-know-whats off. The guys we danced with were really nice, but they kept putting their hands on us. That was creepy, you know."

Megan's parents nod reverentially. Cindi's evening sounds like a nightmare, but it was the right kind of nightmare, the kind Megan's parents approve of because Cindi got plenty of attention and didn't dissolve into subtleties and emotions.

"Then my father called about two in the morning," Cindi adds. "He was drunk somewhere and wanted Ron to pick him up. He started yelling, so Ron hung up and turned off the phone." They talk about Cindi's dad for a while, but every option has been tried or seems impossible. If he causes more trouble, they'll have to report him to the police.

Finally, Cindi asks what Megan did.

Megan says, "I went out and took some pictures."

Cindi looks horrified. Megan nods and tries to look horrified too.

"That's okay," Cindi says. "You always did like to work. I just couldn't stand to work all the time like you do."

"I know," Megan says. She pulls back, as if to take a picture, and sees Cindi in a tightly framed world with her beautiful face fixed, her eyes glazed and looking nowhere. She reaches forward to touch Cindi on the shoulder, but when she does the scene reverses. Cindi's brown hair turns white and her teeth turn black. Megan takes her hand back, and the scene returns to color.

That afternoon Megan has her father take her to the rest home. Her father sits next to his mother and holds her hand. Her skin is yellow-white and sunken in around her bones. There are tubes in her nose and in one wrist, but she acts as if she were an adored child on center stage as she always has, talking to her fingertips as they touch lightly together, going on about nothing.

Megan's father looks helplessly at Megan. She's never seen her grandmother from his point of view. She holds her grandmother's hand while he moves to the back of the room.

Finally, he says, "Come on, let's go. It's time. She won't know if we stayed five minutes or five hours."

Megan pulls away. Tears roll down her grandmother's cheeks though she doesn't seem to know she's crying.

"Honey, are you leaving? Don't leave me here. I miss you,

honey. Thanks for coming to see me. No one ever comes to see me. Now you be a good girl."

"I love you, Grandma," Megan says. She's crying too. She won't see her grandmother again. Her visit is almost over.

"Bye, Mother," her father says and kisses her grandmother's old spotted cheeks.

"You come see me, son. You never come see me."

"I will, Mom." He comes every day.

Megan's father puts his arm around Megan, and they walk out together. Megan is still crying.

"There's nothing to cry about," her father says. "She's an old woman. She's had a good life. It's her time to die."

"I know."

Her father unlocks her door. They drive silently home.

After Megan returns to Vermont, her parents divide up her grandmother's things. They give Megan the china.

"We won't use it anymore," her mother tells her on the phone. "We'll box it up and save it for you."

"Tell Grandma I have it. Tell her I appreciate it."

"She won't understand," her mother insists.

"Please try anyway," Megan begs. Tears roll down her cheeks. She wants to be there. She wants to hold her grandmother's hand and tell her she'll take care of the china, but there are too many obstacles between them.

When her grandmother dies, Megan's parents tell her not to come home for the funeral, there's nothing she can do, though she will be the only grandchild missing.

"By the way," her mother says. "Cindi found out she's pregnant. We're all so happy. Her father already started putting together a crib. He's so handy. I suppose you'll come home to take pictures of the baby?"

Megan tries not to think. "Okay," she says, but she can't go home. She can't get an angle on anything there. There's no time, no space for any perspective to develop. She loses everything she has worked so hard to gain. She wonders if that is what family life is about, if that is why everyone seems to like it.

The Need for Light

IN SPRING IT RAINS WHEN IT isn't snowing. The two compete, like bad children, for your attention. When it rains, the snow melts, so that part of every day there's a soft dripping sound as water runs everywhere, coming off the roof and the hills behind the house, rushing in tiny rivers under and around the house anchored in the backwoods of Vermont. The basement sings like a stone grotto.

Eating breakfast at my dining room table, I watch the sunlight shoot over the mountains, changing everything. Even the clouds, passively, unwillingly, are improved. I think of Michael, my ex-husband, lost forever like a charm from a bracelet. How do people come to be lost from us? Spanish-speakers say *"Adios"* meaning "I commend you to God," acknowledging that each parting may be final. I say "See you" even if I know I'll never see the person again.

I imagine Michael and myself not as we were, but as children standing in the sunlight on a grassy plain next to a river, holding hands, watching the water go by, and I remember how much I loved him. I try not to remember how, one January night when I was three months pregnant and it was fifteen degrees, he chased me out into the snow, locked the door, turned off the lights, and went back to bed. I still wonder what he was thinking as he lay down to sleep, listening to me pounding and crying. Was he thinking anything, or had he left himself, and if so, where had he gone? Since that time I've found that when I leave myself there is nowhere to go.

I put my tea mug down. I stand and wrap myself in a jacket

and scarf, open the front door, taste the cold spring air on the roof of my mouth, and walk toward the nursing home where I work, my head christened by gray-black oaks. I like them best this time of year, their limbs clean and uncluttered against the sky.

I pass my brother Tommy's house where he lives with his dumb wife, Connie, and their son, Charlie, who is three. I rarely visit them because I can't take Connie seriously and can't stop thinking of Charlie as a Mack truck. It would be a cute nickname if the similarities were not so obvious and unpleasant. Charlie is hyperactive and roars through a room like a diesel headed at you on a highway, all metal grimace about to run you down.

In the house across from them our parents rule like base commanders. I could have been a secretary in my family's plumbing business, my father offered, minimum wage under the table, but I said no. Now I direct the day shift. I spend my time looking at the light that I could never see when I lived in my parents' house. Here we believe in light. It heals though it can never cure. All day I move patients in and out of the sun. Even the old blind man, using his fingertips, directs himself along the cold green wall, feeling for the warmth of the rays slanting in.

My boots suck and slurp as I cross a snow-splotched muddy field to the low modern brick building. Inside, the air is hot and dense, scented with disinfectant, rubbing alcohol, and Pepto Bismol. A bent old woman in tennis shoes and red polyester pants raises a veined hand toward me. She is doing her laps, her inspections, drawn down the dim halls and through the bright light of the lobby again and again. If space and love are the same thing, as Einstein said, what crimes or mercies have brought these people here, their lives worn to stumps?

"Help. Help. They're hurting me. Let me go. Help," Mr. Jones, in a wheelchair, protests monotonously.

God will help him soon enough, I believe, drawing him up in a shaft of light, leaving the heavy clamps of bone and metal behind. The presence of God is very strong here with so much impending death.

All day as I wait for patients to chew and swallow what I've spooned into their mouths or rise and shuffle in their walkers, I write letters to Michael in my head. The chronicle of my life is addressed to him though I don't know where he is.

"Mia bambina, mia bambina," Mrs. di Piero cries, pulling at my arm as I hand her blue, white, and yellow pills. Mrs. di Piero has tears on her cheeks, but they're for someone else. I call in an aide, we lift Mrs. di Piero onto the bedpan, she urinates, and we lift her off. *"Ciao, bella,"* I say and blow her a kiss as I leave the room. Sometimes I think this system has been set up so those in charge can feel like saints when they let the pain stop.

What I miss most about Michael is having him in the house, seeing him, and knowing he's all right. I miss the way we knew each other without talking, the way we did things the same. I miss feeling loved and part of something for the first time in my life. What I don't miss is Michael criticizing me to impress my family or popping me on the head when I needed something he didn't know how to give.

Over the years I've watched Tommy's marriage go through its seasonal changes. At first our parents were impressed when Tommy brought Connie home from high school—a small strawberry blonde with her hair curled around her face, her eyes and lips made up so you could see them.

"A cute little thing," my father said after she kissed him on the cheek.

"At least she's got some manners," my mother admitted because Connie answered "Yes, ma'am" and "No, ma'am."

My parents were concerned when halfway through beauty school Connie almost dropped out, but they were optimistic when Tommy talked her into finishing. By the time Tommy finished trade school and started working in the business, Connie had a job at the local beauty shop and was saving for her trousseau. My parents indicated to me—just finished with high school and not sure what to do next—this was the way things should be done.

The morning of the wedding, I was in my room getting ready when Connie came in wearing her white gauze summer wedding dress and crying, a red splotch at the top of her thin white arm. Tommy had gone to pick her up for the ceremony. While they were driving back, Connie talked about how excited she was and how nice everything was going to be and how wonderful his parents had been. Tommy drew further and further into his corner of the car until finally he smashed her on her arm.

"What a thing to do before the wedding," Connie said. How was she going to look with her eyes all swollen and her arm all red?

I got a cold washcloth and sat on the bed close to Connie until she stopped crying and the redness in her eyes and on her arm went down. I had no explanation to offer when she asked, "What kind of a crazy family is this anyway?"

By the end of that summer, I was headed to college to become a nurse.

"We don't see how you're going to make it, a young girl alone," my parents said.

But it was the easiest thing I've ever done. Everyone was eager to help me. I lived in the dorms and went home summers to work in the nursing home as an aide. When I met Michael our sophomore year, he was studying engineering. He had liked wood shop and metal shop in high school, but he had trouble reading and in college couldn't keep up with the physics and the math. I tried to help him until the classes got ahead of me. He dropped out and went to work.

The first time he got angry, I had opened the door to his dark apartment to see him stretched across the bed, sleeping. I decided to surprise him. I picked up the bedspread and put it over his head then straddled his body. He woke up shouting and thrashing, turned, and threw me to the floor. Even when he was up and the lights were on, he couldn't stop shouting. I crouched on the floor, amazed by the damage I had done.

Whenever I came home, Connie would be walking around holding Tommy's arm saying what a wonderful father he was going to be. Tommy and our father would avoid looking at each other as our father sat in his recliner near the television, cracking walnuts and picking the meat out of the shells.

When Connie got involved selling a fancy line of hair and skin products, she found it made her life much more interesting to go door-to-door in the evening visiting the whole town and finding out what went on. She stopped talking about Tommy and having a baby and how wonderful everything was going to be and started working on her figure and going to the city to buy her clothes, so when she went door-to-door in her high heels and slinky dresses and sort of whorishly tasteful little hats, what she had on cost more than what most of her customers had to spend on food for the month. When Connie told the women how these products had just changed her life, they believed her and bought more until Connie was going around in a sporty champagne-colored sedan training new representatives, and Tommy had to eat dinner with our parents again, which went against the whole point of his getting married.

One Sunday just before I graduated, Michael and I found the house on the hill for sale. My father helped with the down payment and offered Michael a job. Before we moved in, we went to a justice of the peace and got married. We told no one until it was over. We didn't want to feel like we were doing it just because it was the right thing to do.

Walking to work, I passed Connie the morning she got into her car wearing her little dress and little hat and drove herself to the pregnancy clinic in the city. She wasn't happy with the news, and for the next seven months let Tommy and anyone who passed by know it, blaming the whole thing on him.

"I told him to control himself," she would say, "but I guess he just couldn't." Before she lost her figure, she would sort of flash her hips around while she said this. Tommy would cringe and scrunch up more than usual while still trying to look tough and being a little proud of what he had done.

After the baby came, Connie got back into her slinky dresses and out on the streets as fast as she could. "I'm home alone in that house all day," she told everyone, "while Tommy's out and around, so I don't see why he can't stay home while I go out and around."

Tommy would take the baby over to our parents' house, and they would tell him what a mistake he'd made and how he'd just have to live with it.

The baby was about six months old when Tommy called in a high school girl from down the street and went out himself. At work he had to listen to our father tell him what a goddamn mess his life was and how he could at least stop drinking and do right by his family. Soon the babysitter turned eighteen. Tommy would invite her over, pull the living room curtains, and not go out. At work Michael had to listen to my father going at Tommy all the time.

The incident about the snow started when I got out of bed and went down to the kitchen to look at the full moon light. I often couldn't sleep. The clouds were passing overhead like in a mystery-thriller movie. I stood at the window thinking a crew from Hollywood might arrive and transform the empty side yard into a place where people were talking and shouting directions at each other, thinking though it would be temporary and the people would disappear again at least something would have happened in the quarter acre of three-foot-deep unbroken snow.

Michael yelled at me, and I went back into our room, but I was afraid to sleep. He was so angry those days working for my family and being nervous about the baby, and I was always staring off, and he was never able to say how he felt.

After a while I snuck out of bed, went into the bathroom, held my arms around myself, and stared at the moon until he started yelling again. I went down the stairs into the living room. When he came after me, I ran outside. When he saw me stop and stare at the moon, even though I was barefoot, and it was freezing, and he was shouting at me, he backed into the house, locked the door, and went upstairs.

When he wouldn't let me in, I went into the barn and huddled in the corner with only my nightgown on. I thought of walking to my parents' house, but it was a long way to go on the dark frozen road, and I didn't want to. I fell asleep dreaming of dry western fields of warm grass the way a prisoner of war dreams of home.

In the morning Michael went to work and left the door unlocked, so I went in. I went upstairs to take a bath, first turning on the electric heat. The sun glazed the room gold, and suddenly I was so warm I cried for how cold I'd been. I lost the baby, but only Michael knew.

When Connie heard about Tommy and the babysitter, she

curtailed her career in cosmetics and stayed home at night. Everyone acted like nothing had happened, which, my mother told me, was the right way to handle it. It wasn't really decent to talk about what had been going on, and what was done was done, and it was all water under the bridge, and didn't Tommy and Connie and the baby make a nice family. My parents couldn't understand what had happened between Michael and me to make him run off like that, what with all Tommy and Connie had been through, and Michael was such a nice young man. I'd nod my head and leave.

At work, I sit with the patients, holding their hands as they tell their broken stories, confusing me with other people. I write their letters or read over and over the ones they've received until their faces become vague and yellow-opal. Some of the other nurses say "Why bother? They can't understand."

This afternoon the patients are in the common room, their wheelchairs and rolling beds arranged in a semicircle, waiting for a Girl Scout troop to arrive. Relaxing in a moment when no one needs me, I realize that though I work in a warehouse for the living dead, no horror show will ever be filmed here. The atmosphere is too quiet and real to interest anyone.

Watching a storm gather, I think *Dear Michael, the light is like a crisis today, splitting the sky from itself. You would like watching it. The silver rays are elegant, precise; but in the end, it is the massive grayness of the clouds that prevails. It reminds me of you as a child, sitting upright in your bed, illuminated by a bolt of light as your father came crashing into your room one night screaming and naked as you told me he did. He finished screaming and slammed the door behind him, and you were left alone in his triumphant cloud of darkness. That is how the light is today as the black clouds finally overtake it.* This is the kind of letter I compose but do not send. I carry it around in my heart like a mother feeling a terrible duty to love a son she knows will be missing in action the rest of his life.

The photographer from the local paper arrives. The leader herds the Scouts in. They bump together in the space cleared for them, nervous and excited about the attention they think they'll be getting, but mostly, the old people are busy with their blankets, their breathing tubes, their IVs.

The girls begin with a few songs everyone knows. The photographer gets what he came for: pictures of the daughters of the town singing to a halo of gray heads. The old people call out songs that were popular generations ago. The girls respond by trying to ad-lib current songs, but they don't know the words to their own songs either. One old woman sings verse after verse of a song no one knows. The girls answer back by jumping bright-colored plastic ropes, whipping the air and beating the ground; then, they sing "We Are the World," their pride recovered.

Finally, the leader calls for a round of taps. I help spread the girls among the patients. They hold hands and sing, linked at last. Everyone is rewarded with sugar cookies and punch. Outside, the storm blows over. The porch and trees are shiny wet and new. The light is clean and coherent.

Walking up the hill to my house, I turn to watch the mountains reflect the setting sun. The silver-lavender haze of bare trees dotted by a few dark evergreens turns peach like an antique print silk dress tossed down, abandoned in this faraway place.

While everyone is busy with their suppers and their fires, I sit at my dining room table studying the mountains' thousand-year-old faces for knowledge of the way things are supposed to be. When the purple light goes, and the hills turn gray and die, I'll turn to the newspaper or the television and the way things are.

I think of the patients, who, like Michael, are stubborn and irritable and can't help the way they are. I find their steady predictable decline easier to live with than the Girl Scouts' quivering potential. My mother always said, "You'll never change anyone." I hadn't wanted to change Michael, only help him be what I thought he was, but he couldn't see what I saw in him. That is why I love the light. It never disappoints me. It is always more beautiful and complex than I can capture or comprehend.

The Boys from This School

HE IS ONE OF THE BOYS FROM this school, so he wears a green military uniform and has a shaved head. He is a freshman, and his name is James. He stands at the door of Kelly's office talking to her after class. As she looks at him, she runs her hand through her short blonde hair. She wonders if her students think she looks attractive or merely curious in the bomber jacket, trousers, and combat boots she wears because she would rather look like them than like the few older female faculty in their skirts and pumps. The students watch her as if she were a changing display, waiting to see what she will do next.

James, in his first essay, wrote about the time his father made him shoot the entire litter of the family cat: *pop,pop,pop.* Now he is writing an essay about the training of Nazi SS troops. In the beginning they are each given a puppy. For several months their puppies are their only friends. At the end of the training, they shoot their puppies; then, they are SS men. James is a sensitive and intelligent student. He gets As on everything he writes. Kelly prides herself on her openness and objectivity even though, in some cases, she wonders if it is morally right.

James is at least six-two with pale blond hair, light blue eyes, a thick dreamy nose and mouth, and acne on his pale skin. He could have been a young Nazi instead of a young ROTC cadet. He wishes he would have been a Nazi. He would have made an excellent Nazi. He would rather kill people than cats, this blue-eyed boy, this perfect gentleman of death, who salutes and says "ma'am" and keeps a knife neatly under his bed and a homemade bomb with half the explosive power of a stick of TNT in his drawer between his underwear and his socks. It occurs to Kelly that he enjoys making bombs the way she enjoys making chocolate chip cookies for her classes. He enjoys blowing things up the way she enjoys keeping things alive—plants, animals, students. Perhaps this is why they get along.

He is looking forward to summer vacation, he says. He just got a letter from his friend in Long Island who is studying to be a minister. They will rappel down his friend's three-story mansion, test out new explosives underneath expensive cars, pursue drug dealers with the intent of scoring not drugs but a kill, and in general, fight the good war. It is the only war there is for him to fight.

Kelly smiles into his eyes and notices the conversation becomes less exciting whenever they veer from the topic of destruction, so they veer from it less and less until he has to go.

Next she writes a letter for a junior who is going on trial the following week for assaulting, with his friends, three students from another college—two males and a female. He is guilty of the crime. That is not in dispute. What will be argued is its seriousness. Was it a felony or not that he broke several ribs with his wild swings and removed the young woman's front tooth? Kelly writes that in class the student is well-behaved and cooperative and at their class party helped her throw two drunker meaner students out.

This is not a reform school Kelly works at. It is a military college where good boys go bad. Kelly works here hoping to change something but knows she probably will not. She works here because she is young and inexperienced and couldn't get another job. She works here because she finds the students interesting and knows the school will go on whether she works here or not. When the students ask why she came, she tells them she is on a cross-cultural exchange from her California way of life. What Kelly has confirmed in this exchange is what she suspected—that men go to war and to colleges like this not because they have to but because they enjoy the camaraderie and sense of purpose it gives to their lives.

Kelly is glad it is Friday. Tonight she will go home and do what she always does on Friday nights in this small New England town where she knows almost no one. She will grade essays. There is no time during the week. There are too many interruptions. She feels the students need her. They give a sense of purpose to her life. On Friday nights no one needs her, so she grades. She has promised her students they can have a party on Saturday night, so on Saturday afternoon she will do the laundry and the dishes and clean the cat box. Her students want to make chocolate chip cookies, drink beer—legal at eighteen with a guardian—and play cards. They enjoy doing these things, and watching them Kelly is both bored and intrigued. She would like some adult companionship at this party, but she doesn't know any adults willing to watch her students play cards. She doesn't know many adults willing to do anything.

After she types the letter, she answers a memo from her department head and outlines the presentation she will make on Sunday evening to the board of trustees. It is a great honor for a first-year teacher such as herself to be able to speak to the board. Normally, the board listens to no one. But she has been hired to direct the freshman composition program and will make a speech about writing across the curriculum. Since it involves the entire university, the board will listen to her. Her department head, who is fifteen years older and has never spoken to the board, will accompany her, mainly so he will appear to be in charge of everything she does.

She looks at her watch then goes to teach her last composition section of the week.

The one student in the room wants to know what they are going to do in class.

"*I* am going to be brilliant," she says, "and *you* are going to be inspired."

When class starts, she asks what should be done about the ongoing Nicaraguan war—the Contras and the Sandinistas.

They shout, "Nuke 'em till they glow!"

When she discusses the role of women in the Sandinista army, one student, Tim, smiling, wide-eyed, shouts, "Keep 'em barefoot and pregnant!"

She asks him to repeat that.

"You got to keep women barefoot and pregnant."

He is still smiling, so she smiles back. "That takes nerve to say in this class," she says.

"I don't care. You got to. Barefoot and pregnant."

She keeps smiling. She doesn't know how else to win this one. Since coming here she often thinks of John Lennon's "Nobody Told Me."

"You're trying to teach us to be Communists," someone in the front row says.

"If I don't, who will?" she replies.

At five o'clock there is one student left in her office. His name is Scott, and he has dark circles under his eyes. He shows Kelly where his roommate scratched him. His roommate is petitioning to get his room changed. His roommate is his best and only friend.

Scott wonders, "Do you ever think of killing yourself, Professor Lockhart?"

"Yes," Kelly answers, smiling at him. For once she is glad that she, on occasion, has considered suicide. It seems it might do someone some good.

Scott wants to drop a class. He is flunking and afraid his father will beat him. Scott is always afraid his father will beat him. This is because his father always does.

She asks Scott how old he is. He says he's twenty-one. She doesn't believe him. He says okay, he's not twenty-one. She tells him he's old enough not to let his father beat him. He says it's not as simple as that. She knows it isn't. She says he's old enough to leave school and be on his own. He says it's not as simple as that. She asks why not. He tells her he's on parole. Scott, with his butch haircut and doe-soft eyes and perfectly developed latissimus dorsi muscles, tells her that three years ago he murdered someone in a fit of rage; then, he tells her he's having trouble in school because he can't hold his pen right. His hand has been broken in so many places he can't move it fast enough to keep up.

Her student Scott, with his doe-soft eyes and perfectly developed latissimus dorsi muscles, stands up and takes off his shirt, showing her a scar that runs from the inside of his elbow to his wrist. He puts his shirt back on and tries to distract her by asking if he would get an A if he took her class. He's not really her student yet, only her advisee. She advises him to see the school therapist. He says he doesn't want to see a therapist because he doesn't want to make baskets or play with dough. She says they only do that in group homes. Then her student Scott has to go to lacrosse practice. She says the exercise will do him good.

"What exercise?" he asks. It's the beginning of the season, and they're having a test on the rules, and he has to write with his goddamn hand.

Kelly wants to hold each of her students and tell them it will be okay. She wants to stroke their backs where their commanding officers have stuffed snow down their shirts and made them stand at attention until it is melted and to stroke their shaved heads where their officers have thumped them with the stones of their large class rings. She wants them not to go to bed alone at night as she does, overcome with desire for comfort. She wants to take away all of their pain and all of her own. Standing in front of them at the chalkboard, she wants to make love to the whole class, spread herself over them and protect them from rejection and harm. But she's only an average-sized woman in a green uniform who can do very little besides give them cookies and easy grades and mildly interesting parties.

Because it is April and there is still snow on the ground, the theme of the party is a luau. Kelly tacks an ad of a young woman posing in a bikini for suntan oil on her front door to mark it.

She is always surprised by how cute her students look in their civilian clothes. One has a bandanna tied around what is left of his hair, making it look wild and punk. Others wear silver-lensed sunglasses. Their cigarettes tremble in their hands as they pass them to each other. They open bottles of beer and juggle canisters of flour and sugar for the cookies. Kelly sets everything out as fast as she can then goes into the living room to play music. She wants to be everything for them except their mothers. They are here to escape their mothers, her department head informed her.

Kelly wants the students to know who she is. She wants someone here to know who she is. She spreads out her collection of magazines--a travel guide to California, a European *Vogue, Pumping Iron II: The Unprecedented Woman,* and a copy of *Young Miss,* which she gets to make up for her missing adolescence. The feature article is "Date Rape." This is the article her students pass around to read. It is the article she read too. Someone says it is interesting; then, the only 4.0 freshman in the university pronounces it's a bunch of crap. The students stop reading the magazine and begin making fun of the women in *Pumping Iron II.*

The party begins to drag. The cookies aren't finished yet, the guy who is supposed to bring the keg hasn't come, and they are all sitting quietly in their chairs, reading. *What do you expect from an English teacher's party?* Kelly thinks. She looks up at the door and smiles as two students from last semester, Lenny and Don, walk in with a big geeky guy and six-packs lined up under their arms. They ask Kelly why are people reading, for Christ's sake, at a party?

The evening begins to move faster. Kelly takes Don and two other students to the convenience store for more beer. With the money left, Don buys a package of Loving Hands gloves.

"Fully-lined," he says, ripping open the bag before they have paid for them. "Complete protection." The woman at the counter does not smile as he dangles the bright yellow tips in her direction. He pulls them on, stretching the cuffs and waving his fingers at himself. "Flexible, long-lasting," he says.

A loving hands party, Kelly thinks.

When they get back, James, the young Nazi, is spread across Kelly's bed. Unfortunately, he's not yet been trained in drinking.

Kelly sits down beside him. She strokes his back. The other students come into the room. They begin going through her things. They like her dresses, they say, examining them. Kelly pulls out a minidress and a pair of striped bloomer pants. She tells Don and Lenny to try them on. They take them and disappear.

Their friend, the geek, is a football player. He puts his arm around Kelly. He thinks she will sleep with him, with anybody, because he has seen her kiss James. He tells her, in a drunken slur, "I could be an English teacher."

"Why do you think that?" Kelly asks. Right now she thinks no one on earth is qualified to be an English teacher, especially herself.

"All you have to do to be an English teacher is to be horny," he says.

Kelly laughs. "Want an earring?" She hands him a large rhinestone one.

"Yeah, I guess." He takes it and puts it on.

Kelly pushes him out of the bedroom and closes the door. She kisses James for a while. "Don't you feel weird?" she asks.

"Yeah."

"I do too," she says, kissing him again. She strokes his back and his shaved head.

"How do you know I love having my back rubbed?" he says.

She doesn't tell him everyone loves to have their backs rubbed. She wants him to believe he is special because right now he is special, no matter how many times they have both done this before.

She hears the students outside her door. She tells them it is okay to come in. She wants them to know she and James still have their clothes on. She wants them to know she is all right. Lenny and Don appear wearing her clothes. Don, in particular, looks smashing in her red dress, red necklace, and red and black bandanna. She loves how he is color-coordinated. The blue in her bloomers matches the blue in Lenny's jacket too. She hugs them. They smile at her and James. Maybe she is all right. Maybe everything will be fine in the morning, and she will still be their teacher. They walk out and close the door behind them.

When it comes time, she tells her student James she doesn't want to be lovers with him. She tells him she wants a boyfriend and not a one-night stand. She has never told anyone this before. He tells her okay and smiles.

She looks at him. How can it be that this young Nazi, her student, nineteen years old, is smiling and saying okay, she doesn't have to do anything with him? Who raised him not to argue with her or throw her aside? How does he live with the complications of what he believes? It is daylight before they go to sleep, and they still have not made love. For the first time in a long time, Kelly is happy.

When she wakes up she can't keep her hands off James, and soon he has a hard-on. Maybe it would be okay to make love now, she thinks, now that they have spent the night together. But James jumps out of bed and stands almost on his toes in the corner of the room, his hands clenched by his sides. Kelly moans a little. She's usually the one to panic and get up. She looks at how perfectly beautiful he is. You would never know, in his ill-fitting uniform, how gracefully his slim muscular legs rise into his flat white groin where now his penis rises red and hard below his long flat stomach; then, his chest begins to develop, the two curved squares of his breasts rising up, branching into the wide armature of his shoulders and upper arms. Before she can ask why he left, he comes back to bed.

She can't not make love to him now, Kelly thinks. Then he says into her ear, "No. You're not going to have a one-night stand this time."

How does she tell this killer of cats and maker of bombs that for the first time in a long time she feels human and loved? She holds him and strokes his back and doesn't realize until later that "Thank you" was all she had to say. He would have understood.

After James leaves, she finds her red dress folded on the living room chair. When she finishes cleaning the house, she notices her bloomer pants and the rhinestone earrings are gone. Lenny and the geek must have worn them back to the dorm. In the afternoon she takes a nap, irons her only good blouse and skirt, reviews her presentation, and takes a shower, glad not to be sticky with come. She checks the map the department head has given her and drives herself to the restaurant where she will be the only woman at the meeting of the board composed mainly of alumni.

He is also one of the boys from this school, only now instead of wearing a green uniform he can afford custom-made suits in any color he wants. He is a trustee, and his name is Frank. At forty-five he is the president of the country's largest advertising firm and a feather in the university's cap, a bad boy made good. He is large, at least six-four, with dark thinning hair and the remnants of rowdy charm. Kelly recognizes him from the school's catalog. He is talking to her department head. They are both belting back Scotch. Kelly hopes she looks invisible in her cream-colored outfit. Her department head introduces her. Kelly shakes Frank's hand.

"Can I get you a drink?" he says.

"No thank you, sir," she says. She is embarrassed because she doesn't consider herself old enough to drink, but Frank doesn't mind, he is still smiling and shaking her hand. She is surprised he wants to know where she is from. Her department head is surprised to hear where she has been.

As the other board members arrive, Kelly circulates. She wishes she were at her party again eating cookies and reading magazines. She wonders where everyone wishes they were. Frank smiles at her a lot. She goes to stand near him. It makes her feel secure. Everyone is standing near Frank. He is so large and magnetic, like a friendly Irish Setter, he makes everyone feel secure. During dinner he keeps smiling at Kelly, but then she feels less secure.

After dinner she escapes to the restroom. On her way back she meets Frank. He is smiling and waiting for her. He tells her they could go drinking or to his room later. Kelly laughs and hits his arm. The oldest trustee, who is about ninety-six, plods by. He lifts his hand toward them. Kelly and Frank salute back. Kelly wants to die.

"Come here. Let's talk," Frank says.

He takes Kelly's hand and goes to a secluded hallway. Kelly likes to talk. She likes to talk and kiss and hold hands. He puts his tongue in her mouth and her hand on his crotch. He has a hard-on. She squirms away.

"Okay, let's get back," he says.

"What?" she asks.

He straightens himself up, and they go back.

To give her presentation, Kelly stands at her table facing the board. Her department head is by her side, but she doesn't look at him. Mainly, she looks at Frank. She is surprised by how easy everything is. Everyone seems human to her now. They laugh at her jokes. When it's over, everyone claps.

Frank asks her to stay for a drink. She says she can't. She kisses him on the cheek.

"Goodnight, Blockhart," he says.

She looks at him. "Only my friends call me that."

"I am your friend. I feel like I've known you a long time."

As she walks down the sidewalk, slipping in the new snow, she turns to see him watching her. She smiles at him and waves goodnight.

When she gets home she puts on her sweat clothes and begins grading. The phone rings, and before she picks it up she knows it is Frank. He is used to getting his way. He wants her to come back. She wants to talk. She asks him why interesting intelligent men are not interested in interesting intelligent women. He tells her he would be if he didn't have a wife.

"Oh," she says.

He has a hard-on, he says.

"I think," she says, "going to this school frees all of you from the last of your ability to love."

"That's probably about right. Now could you come over?"

Kelly asks him about his wife. He loses his hard-on telling her; then, he asks her to describe what she would do if he were there. She describes what she would do if her student James were there. Frank breathes heavily into the phone while he masturbates. He tells her he has come all over his martini underwear; there are white spots on the olives in the glasses.

He tells her he needs a towel. She keeps him talking a few more minutes then says goodnight and hangs up.

She goes to her room to sleep beneath the sleeping bag still piled on her twin bed the way she and James left it that morning. She wonders if James will ever come back or if Frank will ever call; then, she forces herself to go to sleep because tomorrow will be Monday and the boys at her school will expect her to be prepared.

About the Author / Illustrator

photo: Mark Jackson

M. Kaat Toy (Katherine Toy Miller) of Taos, New Mexico, has published a prose poem chapbook, *In a Cosmic Egg* (Finishing Line Press, 2012), a flash fiction book, *Disturbed Sleep* (FutureCycle Press, 2013), novel selections, short stories, flash fiction, prose poetry, creative nonfiction, journalism, scholarly work, and art. Her novel *Madness with Grief* with her illustrations is forthcoming (Livingston Press at the University of West Alabama, 2021). She is completing a book of prose poems with illustrations, *Silences*.

SHANTI ARTS

NATURE ▪ ART ▪ SPIRIT

Please visit us online
to browse our entire book catalog,
including poetry collections and fiction,
books on travel, nature, healing, art,
photography, and more.

Also take a look at our highly
regarded art and literary journal,
Still Point Arts Quarterly, which
may be downloaded for free.

www.shantiarts.com

www.ingramcontent.com/pod-product-compliance
Lightning Source LLC
Chambersburg PA
CBHW051511260626
47162CB00008B/2924